I0677754

BEST MICROFICTION

2024

Series Editors

Meg Pokrass, Gary Fincke

Guest Editor

Grant Faulkner

BEST MICROFICTION 2024
ISBN 978-1-949790-90-0
eISBN 978-1-949790-91-7

First Pelekinesis Printing 2024

For information:

Pelekinesis
112 Harvard Ave #65
Claremont, CA 91711 USA

ISSN 2641-9750

www.pelekinesis.com

*Best
Microfiction
2024*

BEST MICROFICTION
ANTHOLOGY SERIES

Series Editors
Meg Pokrass, Gary Fincke

Guest Editor
Grant Faulkner

Copy Editor
Angeline Schellenberg

Production Editor
Cooper Renner

Layout and Design
Mark Givens

Cover illustration
Terry M. Givens

TABLE OF CONTENTS

ESSAYS & INSIGHTS

Foreword

MEG POKRASS AND GARY FINCKE,
SERIES CO-EDITORS

At six years old, Best Microfiction has established itself, widely read by both writers and a general, international audience. It's sold in bookstores like the beloved Center for Fiction in Brooklyn and has been spotted in the hands of readers worldwide. As always, it has been a delight to pore through nearly one thousand stories submitted by literary magazine editors from around the world.

We have enjoyed working with 2024's Guest Editor Grant Faulkner, whose unique sensibility and deep understanding of the form enhances every page of this year's volume. Each year we feel that our series reflects the hearts and spirits of writers around the world. The idea of offering them a wider, ever more devoted readership is one of the greatest rewards of editing this anthology.

Like the first five volumes, this one continues to demonstrate that we accept and embrace the wild and unclassifiable, and stubbornly refuse to lean toward what may be considered "safe" or "formulaic." Our hats are off to the literary magazines who nominate each year. We feel they are labors of love—tiny islands of humanity in an increasingly robotic landscape—and we continue to support what they do and to celebrate their diversity. As microfiction continues to grow into a form that is garnering a wider readership, we feel so lucky to have been here early, showcasing the very best of the year.

The Art of Microfiction

or
Holding a story in the palm of your hand

GRANT FAULKNER, GUEST EDITOR

My favorite writing assignment as a young creative writing student was Bob Glück's challenge to write a novel in a single page—not to summarize the novel in a blow-by-blow way, but to capture its essence. Similarly, Yasunari Kawabata strove to capture the essence of his Nobel Prize-winning novel, *Snow Country*, in a 12-page version just before his death, "Gleanings from Snow Country."

This is one of the jobs of this form of storytelling known as Microfiction (which Kawabata called "Palm-of-the-Hand stories"): to capture the essence of a story.

So I'm going to try to capture the essence of the singular possibilities of this magical little form in... less than 400 words, the outer boundaries of the form, with a collage of texts from my book, *The Art of Brevity*.

What I love about these tiny stories is that they hold up a different lens to the world—they allow the rags and detritus of the everyday to turn into gems and

3

jewels. Life isn't a round, complete circle, after all—it's shaped by fragments, shards, and pinpricks. It's a collage of snapshots, a collection of the unspoken, a chest full of situations you can't quite get rid of.

Such a tiny form is an invitation to question the very definition of what a story is. A fragment has edges, cracks, seams, and sutures. By being broken apart, it possesses new boundaries, existing in a liminal state. These stories are intimate because they are "in between" things. Microfiction communicates via caesuras and crevices as much as it does through words. There is no asking more, no premise of comprehensiveness, because the form privileges excision over agglomeration.

The magic emerges because of the limitations of the form. Without constraints, we might not feel the piquant pressure that pushes us to find exactly the right word. Each line of a miniature story must carry a symbolic weight that moves the story forward. A writer of brevity has to paint characters in deft brushstrokes, with the keenest of images in such limited space. The writer becomes a vigilant editor, and in looking for what to prune, the writer becomes more attuned to a story's contours, feeling the story in different ways.

In fact, to read such tiny pieces, you have to adjust

your gaze, put on a different mental lens. You have to allow for incoherence and distortions and disconnections. You have to give up your expectations of what a story is supposed to be. Brevity allows us to get close to the unsayable, to know something that is beyond words or the wordless moments words bring us to.

But I didn't have to say all that. I should have just said this: The beauty of a firefly's light is not how it illuminates the world, as the sun does, but in how it illuminates the darkness.

Sometimes it takes the smallest of things to open up the biggest of spaces.

BEST MICROFICTION

Banana

LAILA AMADO

Imagine a backpack, flung off the shoulder of a ten-year-old boy and kicked under his writing desk, straps slouching onto the carpet stained with Sharpie streaks and spilled soda. This is where it will remain, abandoned until the end of the school break.

Imagine a banana. Wedged between the pencil case and a textbook, it lies forgotten at the bottom of that backpack. A leftover from lunch, packed by the boy's mother on the last day of school. If not for the break, it would have been found the next morning—a happy discovery of an extra snack—but, as it is, the banana remains abandoned in the soft, textile darkness. During school break, there is nothing a ten-year-old boy could possibly want in his backpack.

Imagine the weeks fly by while the banana at the bottom of the backpack goes through a series of unavoidable changes. Its bright yellow skin becomes porous and pliable, dull. A few more nights in its hiding place and the first soaking brown spots appear, spread over the softening flesh.

Imagine a mother. It's always the mother who picks up the backpack from the floor on the day her ten-year-old boy goes back to school. She is always the one to stick her hand inside, checking for pens, pencils, an errant lunchbox. Inevitably, her fingers find the banana, plunge through its distended skin and into the soft mush, meet the gooey vulnerability at its core.

Imagine the mother, as she stands in the kitchen, wiping her fingers on a soft crumpled napkin, her nose wrinkled in disgust and pity, watching the yellow school bus roll past the window and take a turn, leaving the cul-de-sac.

Imagine her thinking of the way her husband pecked her on the cheek before leaving for work, casually brushing aside her querying hands. She wonders and worries if this is how he feels about her now—the recoil of pity and disgust—when his fingers meet the soft skin of her belly, the dimpled flesh of her thighs.

Imagine her leaning against the countertop, and the birds outside the kitchen window bob their heads, yellow plumage bright against the barren branches, in mockery or in compassion, she cannot tell.

Laila Amado is a vagabond storyteller who writes in her second language and has recently exchanged her fourth country of residence for the fifth. Her stories have been published or are forthcoming in *Best Small Fictions 2022*, *Cheap Pop*, *Cotton Xenomorph*, *Flash Frog*, and other publications.

A Bird Has Grown Inside My Throat

MILEVA ANASTASIADOU

It started chirping the day my husband got jailed. I thought it came to celebrate my freedom, that it'd soon sing. The bird started talking instead and soon enough I could barely utter a word as if it took over my voice. As if I lost me.

It's obviously a parrot, I tell the doctor. The doctor asks what the bird says. I tell him it says stuff my husband said. As if he had that parrot hidden somewhere and put it inside my mouth before they got him. *Like what?* he asks. I bow my head, remain silent. I don't repeat those words because they hurt, they hurt more than that lump inside my throat. The doctor nods like he understands, then asks me to open my mouth. He checks inside, it takes him long, he takes pictures, he sighs and sighs. As if he can't find me.

He says we'll have to surgically remove it, he shows me the pictures, *not only does it talk like him, but it also looks like him*, I say. The doctor looks away, like he's just thought of something, he says, *we can't take it out, you'll have to spit it out,* and it's my turn to sigh,

11

I wouldn't have kept it in, if I could take it out. As if he read my thoughts, he says it happens often, sometimes we swallow voices, voices that cage us, he'll give me meds that'll make me stronger, that it'll take time. He frowns while he advises me not to get attached to the bird. He means like I did with my husband but he's kind enough to not use those words. I shrug and say I'll do my best but he already looks outside the window. As if he can't see me.

I try to beat the bird that caged me, but it's a strange battle, we're used to birds in cages but not to birds as cages, I scream and scream like the doctor said I should, to silence the bird and get it out, and I get stronger, but freedom doesn't come easy, as if my husband found another way to keep me trapped, caged, even from a distance, and I know now that it may take time, but I will get rid of the bird inside my throat, I'll spit it out and I'll be free.

Mileva Anastasiadou is a neurologist from Athens, Greece and the author of *We Fade With Time* by Alien Buddha Press.

Kin

after Li-Young Lee

MIKKI ARONOFF

Tonight, as all nights, my dog claws and burrows under the covers, whimpers and wrestles head-to-head with day's demons. Is that memory's nightwork? Soon, still. I reach to make sure he's breathing, touch the soft ruff of his neck. He turns on his back, offers his chest for stroking. He wears his heart like an old sweater.

—§—

My cousin excels at packing, arrives lacquered and tanned, bubbling pearled opinions. She reads me like a comic book, fells me with every pressed and folded directive she pulls from her suitcase, along with presents I'll stow with the others in the attic until her next inspection.

—§—

Gram asks for a head skritch while she hems my skirts with her yardstick, croons words in syntax I can't grasp. Mother hangs back in the doorway, scoffs Old World trying for New. Bubbe's teeth clack as she folds the hem, sticks pins, slips into Yiddish into soldiers into sabers into steel. Needles fly from her mouth, thread ties her tongue. What is unspoken rips. Mother winces with every scissored glance. My fingers oily from her mother's scalp.

—§—

Screech of knife, and the sausage on my plate hisses like a neck laid bare. Reek of dung, of hooves chopped at the knuckle. And ravening butchers with latexed hands keep slicing, stuffing. I've had it with dread, its char. Its loneliness like bones.

Mikki Aronoff's work appears in *New World Writing*, *MacQueen's Quinterly*, *Flash Boulevard*, *Bending Genres*, *Milk Candy Review*, *Gone Lawn*, *100 word story*, *Atlas and Alice*, *trampset*, *The Offing*, *Midway Journal*, and elsewhere. She's received Pushcart, Best of the Net, Best Small Fictions, Best American Short Stories, and Best Microfiction nominations.

Dog People

ABBIE BARKER

The evening the neighborhood dogs rebelled, gnawing through fences and tethers, we deserted our wine glasses on back patios and bolted inside. We left rakes, lawnmowers, idle in the grass. We grabbed blunt objects and shivered near windows. We were dog people, all of us, but the way they slouched down the road in a swollen pack, the way they prowled through our garden beds, drove us to cower and hide.

We texted one another. *Did you forget to lock the gate? Did Wesley twist free of his leash?* But no one could explain how they banded together, how they fled in unison. Alone, our dogs were meek. Together they seethed and roamed.

We cracked windows and screamed their names until our throats grew hoarse. We dangled deli meats by our doors. Still, our dogs' eyes drifted. They formed mobs and dug holes. We worried for the neighborhood chickens. We worried for our lawns.

We criticized one another's lack of obedience training. "I always knew Mabel was a bad seed," we said, or "Desmond should've been put down after he mauled the Connors' cat." Our dogs were victims, not aggressors, so we pointed fingers and named ringleaders, accusing the houses to our left of breeding menaces. We targeted the young couples who moved in last month, citing the subtle way our block had shifted, but they blamed long-term residents—anyone living on an unimproved property, spoiling the community aesthetic.

We looked to the sky, the cosmos, but the moon wasn't full that night, just a sliver. As the darkness pressed on, we feared our dogs were too far gone, that it was already too late, so we huddled in corners and assembled barricades. We swallowed pills and drained our whiskey bottles. We dozed to the sound of distant howling.

By morning, we found the dogs resting on stoops and welcome mats, heads bowed, tails wagging, wildness wiped from their eyes. We gradually opened doors and invited them back inside. But from then on, we gripped their leashes tighter, built our fences higher, invested in more training. We isolated every pet, watching for remnants of fierceness. From then on, we watched each other.

Abbie Barker is a writer living with her husband and two kids in New Hampshire. Her flash fiction has appeared in *Cincinnati Review*, *Cutbank*, *Berkeley Fiction Review*, *Pithead Chapel*, *Fractured Lit*, *Superstition Review*, *Whale Road Review*, *Best Microfiction 2022*, and other publications. Read more at abbiebarker.com

Snow, 1979

ALAN BEARD

The first day there I was given over by the foreman to this brash lad, all darts, car and disco. As he showed me how to fit the pit prop together he gave me some chat about girls, about his souped-up car. He made allowances as it was my first day for my incompetence with the handheld crane. The foreman frog-eyed and plump was friendly to me, told me about his sons in the army.

I worked at it, applied myself – not too successfully. One bloke, scrawny, with a big Adam's apple sat on a pile of crates swigging from a plastic cup of coffee. As I did things, wrongly, I could feel his scrutiny.

It snowed later and after our eighth pit prop, our daily quota, we went over to the windows – one whole wall of the place was windows, rattling in their frames. We watched the snow steadily cover everything. The air was white, but if you were out there and looked up a great swirl of black flakes would crowd all vision. A couple of workers, black figures, hurried between the stacks of separate units waiting to be moved, assembled. Left footprints that smudged into fresh white.

A Polish man operating a small lathe nearby said something half intelligible against the echoing and humming background noise. Something about the snow in Poland before the war. He talked fast and accented, and I strained to hear. He spoke of making a hole in the ice to fish, and what kind of fish they caught, and matey, my work colleague, got restless and chomped his teeth a couple of times before talking to me also. How he'd escaped breathalysing, bantered his way out of it.

I nodded at them both in turn. The Polish man was talking about when he was my age; matey about dumping his bird. The snow landed in patches on the window and joined together. The world was softening and lining itself, factory noise seemed to abate, and I heard the lathe operator's voice more clearly, as he talked about Christmas and ice in Poland, before the Nazis appeared on the streets and accumulated.

Alan Beard has published two collections: *Taking Doreen out of the Sky* (Picador, 1999) and *You Don't Have to Say* (Tindal Street Press, 2010). He has stories and flashes in numerous places, most recently in *Leon Literary Review*, *Litro Magazine*, *Fictive Dream*, and *Digbeth Stories*.

Danger Proximal

BRETT BIEBEL

Lana dated this guy who liked cocaine, and no one really liked him. No one but me, anyway. We used to watch HBO late at night and with the lights off, and sometimes it would be action movies or else *Entourage* or *Real Sex* or whatever, and "You make me feel like I'm at a hotel," he said, and his name was Dale. He had a tattoo on his chest. A spider maybe, and I saw it once, when we spilled vodka, and he wiped it up with his shirt instead of a towel. We thought moving around would wake them all up, those assholes sleeping upstairs, and we never said much. Dale and I. Sometimes you don't need to. Sometimes you just watch the light and hear the traffic out on Lyndale, and subscription TV fills your head. Extra sex. Extra profanity. Maybe even a little bit of extra art, and after Lana left him, or, I don't know, could have been the other way around, I found a baggie between the cushions. At night. By myself. Must have been 3AM, and I would have done the drugs if there were any left, but there weren't. There was only a note. "Man," it said, and not another word. There was a drawing of a smile on top of a penis, and I threw that shit away faster than you can spit because what was I gonna do with it? Frame it? Who has the fucking space, and, anyway, I'd already committed it to memory. Dale's smiles. That guilty broken curl you could never really forget.

Brett Biebel is the author of *48 Blitz* (Split/Lip Press, 2020), *Winter Dance Party* (Alternating Current, 2023), *Gridlock* (Cornerstone Press, 2024), and *A Companion to Mason & Dixon* (University of Georgia Press, 2024). He lives and writes in the Quad Cities.

Coyotes, Pelicans, & Prisoners

GUY BIEDERMAN

Neighbors report that a coyote with a mangled leg, hiding in the shrubbery of your complex, growled at a sizeable man who was headed for his Tacoma in the parking lot. From your third-floor unit, you look out at the hills still green in late summer and the busy four lane highway the coyote must've crossed to wind up here. One neighbor walks her leashed dingo towards the shrubbery carrying a knife, another calls the Sheriff saying it should be shot, and a third phones Animal Control insisting the coyote is healing — and residents should just keep all cats and small dogs inside until it leaves. You flip the channel on TV — tune into a local manhunt for an escaped prisoner with a gun. Out the big window, a V-shaped squadron of pelicans flies east. You climb to the roof and make a V with your arms like you did as a kid when wings were sometimes called for, when the line between real and pretend was just beginning to be drawn, when you pondered but-not-for-long your next move.

Guy Biederman is the author of six collections of short prose and poetry including *Translated from the Original: One-inch Punch Fiction* (Black Lawrence Press). He rides a '57 Schwinn, drinks Heart coffee, is hooked on speed bags, but can quit anytime. He lives on a houseboat near Sausalito, California.

Paper Doll

LINDY BILLER

In a drawer, in an envelope, on the little paint-spackled desk—flat-chested, flat-backed, little tabs holding the clothes that cling to paper skin. Yes, I'm flimsy, I know. I feel the way my arms and legs flap when you pick me up from the middle, your thumb and index finger pinching my pencil-dot belly button, where the umbilical cord would've attached if I had been born of flesh and blood and bone. You attach my floral paper dress, my brown paper shoes, you lift my arm and make it wave hello, hinging from the brass pin at my elbow. You switch me to pajamas at bedtime, holding me gentle and breathless as a prayer, as gentle as your mother held you, when you were small, when you could still be held. I know— you can feel in me the potential to crinkle, to bend, to tear. I am fragile. I am not even cardstock. I want to hold your hand and comfort you and wipe your tears, but paper turns to pulp, dissolves with water. I want you to know, I can see how much you care. But don't be timid, don't be so afraid. Pretty things weren't just made to look at, and what am I supposed to be if not yours to destroy?

Lindy Biller's fiction has appeared in numerous journals, including *The Citron Review*, *SmokeLong Quarterly*, *Empty House Press*, *Passages North*, and *Vestal Review*. Her chapbook, *Love at the End of the World*, was published by The Masters Review in 2023. She is the winner of the 2023 Welkin Prize and the 2021 *Fractured Lit* Flash Contest.

Pastels

NICOLE BROGDON

On her last painting, Marisol let me draw a green saguaro in front of the house. Art class was her favorite, especially the waxy pastel crayons. They're not really pastel colors, those crayon sticks. They're vivid. Brown, red, orange—Marisol never used girly colors. Her best drawings were corrals full of horses, trotting near farmhouses. "It's hard to shape their legs right," she said, head bent, shiny black ponytail hanging over her shoulder. She sketched U-shaped horse hooves. Then she bled the color sticks all over the page, smearing them, bold, with her thumb, the pastels shining like Jello. So we licked her drawing. Till Miss Evans said, "Stop! Girls. Lunch is in twenty minutes!" Shaking her head, laughing at us.

I wonder what would have changed if I had gone to school that particular day. I stayed home. With the stomach flu. The shooter let himself into our elementary school through the open side door. Marching, serious, rifles and ammunition packed on his shoulders. Marisol hid in the art room closet with three other kids—they told me that later. Then the

25

colors of the kids get smeared together in my head. Miss Evans was shot too.

When I sleep, I hear Marisol breathing quietly, her breath, cinnamon-sweet, like the churros she shared from her lunchbox. It's like we're having a sleepover now. I draw horses for Marisol, brown and yellow, galloping through waving green grasses on small fast hooves. Running on crooked legs—she's right, the legs are so hard to draw—out from their corrals, past saguaro, towards the sun. Ponies, just running. They're not afraid of anything, those horses.

Nicole Brogdon is an Austin, TX, trauma therapist interested in strugglers and stories, with fiction in *Vestal Review, Flash Frontier, Bending Genres, Bright Flash, SoFloPoJo, Cafe Irreal, 101 Words, Centifictionist, Cleaver*, etc. She was a *SmokeLong* Grand Micro Competition finalist. Twitter: NBrogdonWrites!

Sacrament

MELISSA LLANES BROWNLEE

Pua shifts in the pew as the water and bread are passed out by the chosen boys, her mu'umu'u scratchy and stiff against her skin. She wonders if it will be white or wheat bread. Her mother pinches her on the back of her arm so no one can see as the bishop drones on about stuff she should be paying attention to but doesn't want to, a whispered warning, hot in her ears *no shame me* nails digging, pulling tears from her eyes *no make me take you to da car.* She sits still, her mother's fingers releasing with a last *no make me do dat again, girl,* her mother's eyes fire, a smile wide across her face as she checks to make sure no one heard her. Pua knows no one cares. She's sure all the other kids' arms are scratched black and blue too, their brown skin hiding all sins. The bread and water come to her row, her brother so proud in his aloha shirt and slacks, holding the tray and walking down the row. She hopes he drops it before he gets to her so he's the one who gets it and not her. He stops in front of their mother, her smile reaching her eyes. Carefully she lifts the piece of wheat bread and places it in her wide mouth, her lips close as she

27

chews and swallows. Her fingers curve around one of the tiny little cups filled with water, her nails flashing red, lifting it slowly to her lips, sipping it, savoring the moment, before placing the empty cup back. Her brother moves to her, his smile matching their mother's and Pua prays as she chooses her piece of brown bread, her mother's eyes hard on her.

Melissa Llanes Brownlee (she/her), a native Hawaiian writer living in Japan, has work published and forthcoming in *CRAFT, swamp pink, Pinch, Moon City Review* and *The Threepenny Review*. Read *Hard Skin* from Juventud Press and *Kahi and Lua* from Alien Buddha. She tweets @lumchanmfa and talks story at melissallanesbrownlee.com

Lesson One: Simona

KATI BUMBERA

Simona is a mountain. She is tall. She speaks with an accent.

Where are you from, Simona? I am the daughter of continental plates. My parents argued when I was born. I fled the desert to go to school. The children laugh. There's distant thunder.

Simona writes an essay. What do you want, Simona? I want to see the sea. Simona graduates with honours. The teacher laughs. You are a mountain, Simona. They will drill tunnels through your belly. They'll smear hot asphalt on your face.

They'll move the sea just out of your reach.

Simona rents a small apartment. She goes to work in a big city. Her boss owns all the summer months. He rejects Simona's leave request. He says, you are a mountain, Simona. Also, your forest is on fire. Her colleagues laugh. There's distant thunder.

Simona has a tall, American boyfriend.

Simona gives birth to a small rock. It's carried away by the river.

Simona is taken to hospital. The doctors don't know what's wrong with her. She attracts lightning. She coughs up lava. The doctors tell her it's her fault. You are a mountain, Simona. Your guts are made of lodestone. It broke our scanner. There's nothing we can do.

One night, a woman comes to see her. She says, hello, Simona. I am a ghost. I wear these long skirts, these high-heeled boots. They weren't made for hiking. I came too early. Before my time. They told me that the world was flat. They tried to lock me in staid rooms. But I still climbed you. And from your heights, I saw the sea. I saw the thunder, the avalanches. I am dead now. But you, Simona, are a mountain.

Simona survives, encircled by summer. It never ends. Her boss gets rich. There's constant thunder. Simona is a mountain. She's everyone's playground and refuge. But her forest burns all the time.

Her son sends her a postcard from the sea.

Simona's old. She lives in a nursing home. Strangers come and go every day. Simona wants to be alone. At night, a cat sits by her window. She sees desert stars in the cat's eyes. She sees the storms, the avalanches. She sees the woman in her soaked skirts. She sees the sailors, steering by lodestone in the dark.

Simona knows she is a mountain.

There's distant thunder.

Kati Bumbera loves to hike in the mountains with a notebook in her backpack. She's a video game writer by day and has also published short fiction in various online magazines. Snow and winter are her favourite things to write about. She lives in France.

Blackberry Nights

MYNA CHANG

You watched your grandmother cut back the blackberry canes every spring, saw how she bore the thorns and the loss. *This is love*, she said, when her skin split and her blood dripped into the soil. After you understood the source of the bramble's rampant growth, you swore off legacy and family obligation and left, never to return, never to sacrifice the fruit of your own marrow. Now though, with summer on the wane, your veins swell to bursting and you think of your grandmother, the paperbark of her skin and the glint of her teeth fierce and sharp under the kindred moon and you swear to god you'd kill for a drop of her hedgerow wine, another taste of that blackberry night. So you return to the canes, take up the shears and the paring knife. You love. And you bleed.

Hometown Johnnies

MYNA CHANG

It was the night Johnny came back to town, one of those pent-up summer nights when the sky trembled heavy with unshed moisture, weighing us down, the burden of it pressing us into the dust, and we wanted to scream *let go!* but heaven wouldn't unleash that water, held it fist-tight, just out of reach, pushing the young people to burst and the old people to beg.

Someone said Johnny came in on the bus, he hitch-hiked, Johnny cruised into town in a candy-apple Mustang, sweet as punch. He stood in his momma's driveway, outside the diner, on the tracks by the overpass. Someone saw him walking down Main Street, eddies of powdered grit swirling in his wake.

It was the night of the harvest moon, beams breaking through the clouds, spotlighting the wheat stubble, casting shadows sharp across the shredded stalks and the ruts. Johnny bought a six-pack at the gas station, a fifth of bourbon at the liquor store, a coffee at the donut shop, paying whatever he had for a chance at deliverance.

They said he'd been working on an oil rig, he'd enlisted in the army, he'd gone to California. Johnny followed the rain to places made of more than dirt, where droplets flew wild in the night, free from sacrifice and prayer. He'd gone to swim in the ocean, to wade in a creek, to dive headfirst into an impossible pool of crystal blue. They said he'd gone to make his way.

It was like so many other nights when the sky teased and the ground ached, like so many other Johnnies caught in the between, consumed. We heard he lost an arm in a thresher, he shot a man in Tulsa, he struck it rich in Vegas. Johnny came home in a leather jacket, a three-piece suit, a star-striped box. His momma didn't cry, but his daddy did, standing smack in the middle of the VFW parking lot, the high school parking lot, the Methodist parking lot, salting the hardpack earth under that brutal moon, bargaining with that bitter sky.

It was the night we searched everywhere, hoping to see Johnny around the next corner, wondering if our own sky would ever let go, or if we, too, might burst before we made our way through the drought.

Originally published in Middle House Review.

Myna Chang is the author of *The Potential of Radio and Rain* (CutBank Books). Her writing has been selected for *Flash Fiction America*, *Best Small Fictions*, and CRAFT. She has won the Lascaux Prize in Creative Nonfiction and the New Millennium Award in Flash Fiction. More at https://mynachang.com

Make Me Yours

CHRISTINE H. CHEN

When I was a little girl, I followed Ah Ma like a shadow. *Go away*, she yelled, *you're blocking the sun* when I pulled on her sleeve. Her hair was a canopy of black sky with silver stars. I grabbed onto one end. Ah Ma shook me off like an annoying gnat. In the process, I snatched a few strands of her hair I taped on my head. It wasn't enough. I asked for her skin. She said, I could never have her beautiful peachy skin. I scratched her face, glued her cells onto mine. *You're a monster*, she said. She chased me with a broom, screaming, *you have nothing of mine!* She pulled a mail-order catalogue, and waved it in front of me, *see this page here, I could order a perfect daughter if I wanted to!* On the glossy sheet, a porcelain Chinese doll for a $100 that looked like a glittery machine with her traditional gold and silver embroidered *qi pao*, motorized noodle arms and legs. I finally understood. I grabbed a screwdriver from Ba's toolbox, and rushed after Ah Ma, yelping, *let me open your chest and check your heart!* We ran in loops until we lost our breath, our head, our mind, until our parts couldn't be nailed back together.

Maxillectomy

Christine H. Chen

The nurses gather around Ah Ma who's floating inside the green gown, tubed to beeping machines, getting her blood drawn from her difficult to find vein, and giving praise, *good job* to the nurse who says, *aww your mom is so cute* to the daughter who's remembering Ah Ma's slap on her face when she missed a spot of dust on the windowsill, *you're sloppy*, *you're dumb*, when she brought home a less than perfect score in a math exam, Ma's clapping and cruel laughs after a goose bit her butt, so when the nurses announce, *we're wheeling your mom in, wanna give her a hug*, her words shoot out, *no, we're not touchy people*, and she crosses her arms until after the surgery, when she sees Ah Ma's swollen mouth that's never kissed her, Ma's hand limp and begging, she takes the cup and the straw, leans close to her mother's face, *here's some water.*

Born in Hong Kong and raised in Madagascar before settling in Boston where she worked as a chemist, Christine H. Chen has published fiction in *SmokeLong Quarterly*, *Time & Space Magazine*, *Wigleaf* Top 50, and elsewhere. She is a recipient of the 2022 Mass Cultural Council Artist Fellowship. www.christinehchen.com

A little martyrdom

ZOA COUDRET

There is a breath-long moment before the needle jabs when you think, *Maybe the piercer will nick a vital artery, maybe this will send me to hell* & you wonder if you are only doing this because your partner has broken up with you & you want to choose the way you hurt, which it really does as metal slides through skin, pain stuns nostril to brain & you suffer, Christlike for a few seconds—long enough to wonder *Would Jesus have gotten a nose ring if there'd been a piercing shop in Nazareth? Definitely a tattoo, perhaps a "MOM" heart or a realistic portrait of his father, burning bush, all black & grey, flames rising from bicep to shoulder*—before your eyes clench & tears flow like holy water on a baby's bald head, the little blood you lost will replenish, unlike your self-esteem when a pale selfie reveals the niobium bar stuck through the bridge of your nose, misplaced stigmata, you wish someone were here to pose with you to make your ex jealous, make them think you're thriving, because you crave their regret, want them to see you strong and unbothered, desire so much more than what a little piece of metal can give.

Zoa Coudret (she/her) is a queer & trans writer, artist, & designer.

Its Meanness to the World

JON DOUGHBOY

Henry David is thinking about Mrs. Emerson and playing with himself as he surveys his beans. He wants to sojourn into and out of and into and out of Lidian in an act of carnal transcendence but he has beans to tend, ants to watch, an image to maintain. *The Dial* is expecting another travelogue chock full of his signature pithy digs at this young nation's nascent consumerism. The Walden Gift Shop is waiting for his next batch of genuine Thoreau pencils. The taxman is still on his ass about his disobedience and no matter how many hankies he goes through, there's always a hunk of tubercular phlegm hardening in his beard. The waters of the pond are calm this evening, quiet, desperate. Where is this fucking dawn, he thinks. But the night is long and growing longer, eight weeks long, eightscore, an interminable New England night, and Henry David goes mad in it, madder than usual, his beans withering without the sun, his cock withering without Lidian, his life a-wither. He looks up at the star-pebbled sky and hark! You can hear his hammer dismantling his home, deliberately, for life, in the end, drives him into the corner despite his Spartan sturdiness. His home comes undone too easily. The dawn comes with it. Lidian, O Lidian, O have you seen Lidian! Around the pond he walks, the path to the civilized world clear now thanks to the morning star. He enters the gift shop, confronting walls of hats and tee shirts and onesies and mugs stamped with his aphorisms and maybe this is an enterprise he should beware of but according to the cashier, yes, they're hiring, and he's tired of this incredible dullness, tired, so tired, of being alone.

Mulberries

JON DOUGHBOY

June in the rustbelt and we're raving drunkenly down the street trying to catch mulberries in our mouths as they fall, chomp chomp chomp their bloody juice and save them from the sidewalk, from smearing into oblivion in the bottom of someone's uncaring shoe or some mangy dog's concrete-coarsened paw pad, except our shrinks tell us we're sane and our sponsors tell us we're sober and that mange is easy to cure but we don't care, we're ravenous, we're eating salads of toxic algae blooms we skimmed off the surface of this mighty nation's Great Lakes and fruit cocktails from berries scrounged off trees and bushes flowering in the pestilent ruins of our once great industries and here's one, a mulberry, gulp, except it tastes like spring not summer, like pollen and mudslides and black flies sucking our blood in the U.P. and gulp, another one, and this one too is unseasonably flavored, tastes of winter, knitting needles clacking in a brick rowhouse, Netflix ta-dumming into poorly-written sit-com life, and the fog isn't Sandburg's coming on little cat feet, it's not even fog, it's a smog of volatile organic compounds belched out of the cracker plant, but that's ok, we don't mind, we're volatile organic compounds ourselves, like recognizes like, our necks heavily adorned with fordite pendants the size of Buick Electras and our teeth are made of COR-TEN steel weathered brown and gulp, this one is fall, of course, for nature and narratives love a pattern, and that's ok because we're fall people, we tell ourselves, our sponsors, our shrinks, we're autumnal creatures, citizens of a decadent empire, and it tastes like papery leaves like Rilke like a pigskin bouncing off the hard November-frosted earth like a shock full of fodder like a family trampled on Black Friday like you and me in our brilliant senescence catching mulberries and raving drunkenly down the street in the rustbelt in June.

Jon Doughboy is an installation of art for art's sake. Take a tour @doughboywrites

After Steady Work Dries Up, the Aging B-Movie Queen Reconsiders *Fright Night*

ALYSON MOSQUERA DUTEMPLE

The movie is a horror film. The movie is in a theater, at night. There are strangers in the theater. Your child is among the strangers, slouching, in a seat much too close to the screen. Your child is accompanied by a "friend from school." You do not know the friend. The movie features gratuitous violence, gratuitous everything, the kind of gratuity that made you famous, the kind of gratuity you now fear can give a person ideas. There's artery-clogging fat in the popcorn. There's processed corn syrup in the drinks. There's an overdue co-pay at the pediatrician's and too high a balance on the credit card your child has borrowed from you. There's no more waiving of late fees. The movie ticket costs 15.00. The concessions cost 15.00. The parking garage costs 15.00. Your child doesn't care about the costs of things, hasn't learned the value of a dollar. Your child's shoulders are constantly hunched. Your child is growing up crooked. Your child doesn't care about good posture, doesn't respond when you try to talk in the evenings after work (when you say *how was school today, did the counselor call you into the office, did the kids call you that name again, the one that makes you feel that way, did you tell anyone else about what's happening to you, are you avoiding social media like the doctor recommended*). Your child is not avoiding social media. Your child has show biz aspirations. On your feed, a selfie of your child appears, a photo from within the theater just before the lights go down. The seats are stadium-style, deep, private. The friend's hand is gripping your child's shoulder. In the dim lighting, the hand looks older than you would have expected, alarmingly weathered and pinky-ringed. Your child is grinning wide, so wide, that you can see your child is not wearing the orthodontic retainer you always fight about. Your child's smile has cost more than your car. Your child's smile has cost more than you could ever calculate. Your child's smile costs and costs. The selfie disappears moments after you heart it.

Alyson Mosquera Dutemple is a writer from New Jersey with an MFA from the Program for Writers at Warren Wilson College. Her story collection was a runner-up for the 2022 Flannery O'Connor Award for Short Fiction. Find her at alysondutemple.com

Tangerine

ALLISON FIELD BELL

I tell the story beside a fire in the Organs, the peaks a dark mass at my back. "I tried to drown myself in a hot tub," I say. No moon, just a shock of stars. My sister should be here, but she's forever in California, and I'm in New Mexico, a plate of pasta ignored in my lap.

My lover is across from me, sauce caked to his beard like blood. Today, he identified life for me: birds, lizards, juniper, yucca. He worships what survives. Even a crust of dirt he finds remarkable. Now, deep in on the whiskey, he's talking about climate change, politics, capitalism, fascism.

"I tried to drown myself," I say again. "Narcissism," I say, laughing, hand over heart like a pledge. But he isn't laughing and suddenly I'm back there with her.

Halloween, high school, Tinker Bell glittering the crowd. Think happy thoughts! The pale blue cotton shirt and sparkling tights, the look of them wet and clinging like a new layer of skin. A silly party—hers—and water all around, and all night. Hot tub, pool: tiptoeing between, wings dripping. Later, the sealed cover. Body floating there in the dark.

Her body and not my body.

That Zeppelin song dissolving, *Tangerine, Tangerine.* The words in my mouth like actual fruit, solid and sweet and fleeting: *she was my queen, a thousand years between.*

My lover has his arms around me now, the fire collapsed into a jeweled pit of light. "Sorry," he's saying. "Your sister, I didn't know. I'm sorry."

Allison Field Bell is originally from northern California but has spent most of her adult life in the desert. She is currently pursuing her PhD at the University of Utah, and she has an MFA from New Mexico State University. Find her words at allisonfieldbell.com

Father

ALEXANDRA FÖSSINGER

It is not true that the dead do not age. I see my father often, on the street, the way he would look now, older, with slower movements; he has lost some weight, his face has sunk in, it has a darker expression; his once thick hair has thinned out and turned completely white.

He will pause sometimes, slightly bewildered, unsure of where he is. Perhaps that comes to those who never quite left a place, never quite reached another. Only a few minutes ago I looked down on him from the window of my studio. He stopped at the parking place for a few seconds and closed his coat against the cold, before moving on. Strangely enough, he did not raise his head. He would not have greeted me, the dead never acknowledge the living, but I thought he would look up anyway. He might have forgotten.

Alexandra Fössinger is an exophonic writer from Italy and the author of the poetry collections *Contrapasso* (Cephalopress, 2022) and *Recount and Prophecy* (Alien Buddha Press, 2024). Her poems are published in numerous journals including *Gyroscope Review*, *Tears in the Fence*, *The High Window*, *Oyster River Pages*, *Feral*, and *Tokyo Poetry Journal*.

Chopsticks

JEFF FRIEDMAN

How he loved remembering that she had been in love with him, kissing him suddenly while they sat at the piano, playing Chopsticks together. She didn't remember that: kissing him or being in love. *I would never have played Chopsticks, or any other song with you. I never learned to play the piano,* she said. He took her hands in his and looked into her eyes. *We were lovers,* he said. *I just met you,* she answered. He led her to the piano and helped her sit down. *We've been married a long time,* he said, taking the spot next to her. She closed her eyes, thinking about what he had just told her, but when she thought about lying down in the bedroom, she couldn't picture him beside her. When she thought about the living room, he was not in it. Nor was he with her when she walked the neighborhood, stopping to admire the purple flowers and the Burning Bushes. Nor could she place him in the garden. Nor could she feel his lips kissing her tenderly on the cheek. As he began to play Chopsticks, her hands moved up and down too, but didn't touch the keys.

Jeff Friedman has published ten collections of poetry and prose and has collaborated on two books of translations. His most recent collection, *Ashes in Paradise*, has just been published by Madhat Press. He has received an NEA Literature Translation Fellowship and numerous other awards.

Bones, Only Bones
A Skeleton Triptych

FRANCES GAPPER

1.

A skeleton who doesn't have a partner lies down on the beach next to a jellyfish and whistles an empty-chested sigh. "Food became hard to digest, so I stopped eating."

"Lucky me, I have only one orifice," says the jellyfish. "Stuff in, waste out." But its polite pipe is drowned by the skeleton's clatter-chatter: "My idol, whose name I don't recall. Her grave is awkwardly situated, on a hill. She's taking her time decaying. I can't hang around indefinitely..."

The jellyfish dreams of catching mini shrimp in ocean depths. When it wakes, the skeleton is still talking. "Don't you ever shut up?" the jellyfish asks.

Clish clash. "I believe in everlasting love. Although I never found it. When young, my acted-upon impulses caused offence, so I learned not to act upon impulse. Haha."

Wish wash, the jellyfish thinks one moment you're beautiful and graceful, next moment cast up on the beach, a lump of jelly. Oceanic sadness.

The skeleton wants to put its hand in the jellyfish. "If you do that, I'll die," says the jellyfish.

"Romantic, though."

"Not in a nice way."

Hish hush, the tide comes in. "Ow!" – the skeleton leaps up. The jellyfish is lifted and cradled. "Goodbye!" it calls.

2.

A skeleton can't stop doom scrolling. It makes an appointment to see a life coach who suggests hypnotherapy. "No thank you," says the skeleton.

"Was your death traumatic?"

"No more so than anyone else's."

3.

When you're a skeleton, you take a nap on your parents' grave. The grave is kind to bones, unlike your orthopedic mattress.

When you're a skeleton lying on a grave, other cemetery visitors point and exclaim. "Look! How weird. Perhaps badgers dug it up."

When badgers dig up graves, they scavenge gold rings from arthritic joints and sell them in the Jewellery Quarter, to fund political fightback campaigns. Badgers object to being stupidly scapegoated for bovine tuberculosis. They've started to hate humans.

When wild creatures learn to hate, it's the End Times.

When it's the End Times, you visit your parents' grave and wait till dusk. At dusk they climb out, shrieking. Dad makes 'jokes' (see above, parts 1 and 2). Mum keeps touching your skull – "It's beautiful!"

Frances Gapper's stories have been published in three previous *Best Microfiction* anthologies and online in places including *New Flash Fiction Review, Splonk, Forge, Gooseberry Pie, Wigleaf, trampset, 100 Word Story, Switch, The Dribble Drabble Review, Twin Pies, Janus, Fictive Dream.*

Lovesong for the 0% Finance King Size Mattress

JO GATFORD

There is only one sharp knife in this damn kitchen and I can take the whole world as a personal insult but you can slice vegetables without drawing blood; live your entire life without once doing a tax return; can stand in the sun the way a body was meant to and not burn deep enough to bruise.

Remember when we disemboweled our mattress, broken backed and heavy as a corpse—four-hundred-and-sixty-seven springs cut out one by one until our hands turned rusty blister purple—and I fed a list of songs I knew you'd hate through the tin can speakers of my phone just so you'd have something else to be angry about?

We sprawled its guts out all over the patio: ten years of skin, sweat, and dust mites clouding into the air. And maybe it wasn't the moment to get sentimental about the fevers and the breastfeeding and the fucking, and god, how long it took to pay off, even with zero interest—financial babies before the real babies came—but it feels like a betrayal to the new mattress as we lie awake past midnight, the freezer buzzing like it's full of crickets, and I say:

Remember when we cut a mattress into pieces—what were we thinking? I let you take the knife, I took the scissors. And you know I would bury a body with you, right?

Because we are closest this way; skin and linen sliding past one another while we wait for the rain to come, waiting for the exhale of the sky, still so solstice bright the birds don't even know it's night.

Give us ten more years and we'll be experts on each other, but for now we need to wear a new groove into the middle of the bed.

Jo Gatford is a short writer who writes short things. Her work has most recently been published by *The Oxford Prize*, *Stanchion*, *The Fiction Desk* and *Cease, Cows*. Some of her writing wins prizes. She is also a novelist, poet and scriptwriter, and edits other people's words for her supper.

Lucky

KATE GEHAN

The dead grandmothers want you to send up a flare
when you're in need. Sob them every hormonal song
from your electric, changeling body. Zap za-zing!
Don't bother with deep breathing sweetheart! Ruin
something as a signal. Burn the crust of the key lime
pie or fall asleep in a hammock instead of consoling
a distraught man and they'll show up wild—leopard-
print mini-skirts, camisoles, unkempt hair long and
dyed turquoise—no pantyhose or flat-ironed blonde
bobs for these dames. The dead grandmothers are
fully in love with themselves because it's high time.
They have each other now. They have themselves.
They don't care where the grandfathers have gone.
They're interested in cheesecake and a French 75.

If you're fourteen they'll snuggle up on the sectional
beside you and watch trash television, blush at the
pony-tailed men with burly arms on dating shows,
tsk tsk over your high school crush who can't match
his socks, let alone text you back. The dead grandmothers will throw 4 am dance parties and tattoo you
on the bathroom floor. If you're forty-eight they'll

peer in the bathroom vanity and tell you to stop worrying about smile-lines. Honey, get a younger lover and book a Caribbean trip. Turn your face towards the heat.

While you sleep the dead grandmothers meet themselves in the forest and flirt, slip themselves free. They don't waste time sucking up car exhaust at Newark airport waiting for a late lover. They don't fold themselves into silver sedans to kiss men through a cloud of cologne and Winston smoke anymore. They don't even need patience and one day you'll understand irrelevance too. The dead grandmothers slide and soak into the fragrant night to take flight on the backs of insects whose names you can't be bothered to learn.

Kate Gehan's short story collection, *The Girl and The Fox Pirate*, was published in 2018 by Mojave River Press. Her writing appears in Alan Squire Publishing's *Already Gone: 40 Stories of Running Away* anthology, *Smokelong Quarterly*, *Mom Egg Review*, *McSweeney's Internet Tendency*, *Split Lip Magazine*, and *Literary Mama*, among others.

Lace in Your Hands

LYDIA GWYN

When I hear you brother, trembling in your grave, I imagine you alive. Sharp as black pepper. I catch you in the scent of gunpowder, in tunes whistled from someone's mouth. In limbs of snow waiting like brides in the woods.

Once, we went together on our bellies with pens and paper to the underworld. We saw all the stars in tiny bowls on the side of the road. Tasted the grammar of ashes. But I returned alone, stained and cold, balled in a fist. For a long time, there was a braid of anchors inside me.

You would love my children. My daughter's style, her fierceness on a skateboard. My son's big heart. He's the kind of kid who gives all his birthday money away. And his face is a near replica of yours.

I try to remember the sound of your voice, and it comes to me as a sensation in my own throat. A mushroom growing in the darkness, aching like a phantom limb flung from the body.

Ours was a game written in chalk on a wall. A hill of white clover. You might shut the lid of your lunch box and return with these images. The tarmac teeming with ants. You, on top of the roof, unable to climb back down. Stuck with tree bark like lace in your hands. Our mother's felt hat, dropped in the school hallway after we argued over which of us would wear it to class that day.

The day you made a mist of yourself, you moved across the grass, down the field, into the leaves. You turned to fire and blossoms and morning school buses. Lights flashing in the fog above the road. Three steps up, three steps down. This is how to travel across time. Across my hair still wet from the shower. Into the house of constant prayer inside my head.

Give me your to-do list dotted with rain. The music from behind your door. Your muffled words. My son dreams of you in his room sometimes. You sit behind the drum set and glow like the moon.

Lydia Gwyn is the author of the flash fiction collections: *You'll Never Find Another* (2021, Matter Press) and *Tiny Doors* (2018, Another New Calligraphy). Her work has appeared or is forthcoming in *F(r)iction*, *Midway Journal*, *Anti-Heroin Chic*, *The Florida Review*, *New World Writing Quarterly*, and others. She lives with her family in East Tennessee and works as an instruction librarian at East Tennessee State University.

Our Mothers

L Mari Harris

slow dance to sad songs. buy our first training bras.
lose their cool. let us try on their Saturday-night clothes,
fill our arms with bracelets, spray Jungle Gardenia
behind our ears. complain about our fathers. insist we
develop hard hearts. *You'll thank me later.* sometimes
forget we're in the same room. tell us we can't reach
the stars, but we can have the clouds below. pick up
extra shifts to pay the light bill. ask us to rub their
sore feet. warn us not to get into cars with strangers.
*Don't fall for that missing dog trick. Second oldest trick in
the book.* What's the first trick? *When he tells you he's not
going anywhere.* cut the green part off the food-bank
bologna. watch *Law & Order* marathons late into the
night, the *dun dun* lulling us to sleep. teach us how to
do our own laundry, how to smile at the landlord as
we hand over the short check. never cut us any slack.
make it all feel like too much. tell us they're sorry
they're so cynical. We look it up: *distrustful; suspicious.*
miss our fathers. cry out it's too late for them, but
we'd better learn now how to throw the first punch,
how to let everyone know we're not to be messed with.
are bursting at the seams. are fraying at the edges. are
coming apart.

Something Inside Us Rises Up

L MARI HARRIS

Out on the gravel road that T-bones the highway, we drop our tailgates. Watch the chicken trucks rumble past.

We sip Cherry Limeades, brush French fry salt from our bare legs. The boys devour their sandwiches in three bites, smack their lips. We laugh high and long, wrestle them so we can grab their sun-warmed arms.

White feathers catch and ride the wind when the trucks roar by. They snag in the scrub along the ditch and come to rest in the truck beds and by the tires. We search for the unblemished feathers, glossy and white as sugar, and tuck them in our ponytails.

The boys tangle their thick fingers in our chicken-feather hair. Pull us close. We try to outdo each other with the places we'll move to one day: *Bahamas or California, live on the beach; Montana, become fishing guides and live in big log cabins.* Anywhere but here.

Our voices trail off.

We change the subject, shout our bets as more hawks line up equidistant along the powerlines. So still. Like statues.

If we sit long enough, a chicken or two will escape its cage as a truck speeds past, its chicken-tumble flight taking it just high enough, just far enough, to land in the ditch or the edge of the farmer's field.

They always flail around a little in the weeds and water grass, then start pecking at the dirt like nothing ever happened. If you didn't know better, you'd swear the chickens had always lived by the side of the highway.

Our eyes lock onto the hawks.

We hold our breath.

Then, just like that, a hawk pitches forward. Nose-dives. A hoarse scream as it rights itself and the talons extend.

Something inside us rises up. We cheer and fist bump.

If you didn't know better, you'd swear we didn't understand the chickens' side of the story.

L Mari Harris's stories have been chosen for the *Wigleaf* Top 50 and *Best Microfiction*. She lives in the Ozarks and is currently at work on a linked collection of flash fiction about her home state. Follow her @LMariHarris and read more of her work at lmariharris.wordpress.com

Exorcism

SARA HENRY PAOLOZZI

When the priest leaves, I talk to the demon living under my skin. I speak into the holy-watered dark.

I say, "That guy was an asshole."

I tell her she can stay as long as she likes. I tell her not to worry, God is on our side. I tell her she was a child once. I tell her that the very people who created her are trying to cast her out. I tell her that I would rather die than have never met her. I tell her we were meant to be. I tell her to watch the scene in Goodwill Hunting when Robin Williams tells Matt Damon it wasn't his fault. I tell her to watch it again. I tell her that she scares people because the truth is scary. I tell her she scares me too, that I am scared of the truth too. I tell her that I love her. I tell her that, someday, people will say that this is a beautiful story. I tell her they just need to see the ending to understand that it was beautiful from the beginning. I tell her that I'm listening, whenever she's ready to speak. I tell her I'll wait for as long as it takes, that I'm here, arms open, hands burning.

Sara Henry Paolozzi's work has appeared in *The Cortland Review*, *Autofocus*, *Booth*, *Adroit Journal*, and elsewhere. She lives in Austin, Texas, where she's at work on her first novel. You can find her on Twitter at Sara_Paolozzi

The morendo

Yedidyah Herrero

One morning I awoke to find all the birds gone. No mockingbirds speaking in tongues. No mourning doves stretching their bassoons. No pigeon flocks turning like galleons in the wind. All gone, replaced by insects grown into their berths, from hoppy wee finch size to terrible large eagles and somewhere, perhaps, portly ostrich-tall locusts. Gone too their solo songs, the trills, the strains, the melodies, and refrains deposed by a stridulent buzz, a collective hum, the eternal friction of mechanic leg on hollow belly. It resonated in my skull with a sympathetic vibration that rattled my thoughts from signal to noise. I asked the men in my village McDonalds, where are the birds? What birds, they asked. I asked the Book, but the Book's OS had gone extinct. Ai-ai-ai, I cried, and AI answered, I don't know that word, bird. So I asked my pouch-mate, what of the plumage of many colors, what of the blithe spirit, what of the light-winged Dryad of the trees and she said, don't you think that was always too much to ask?

Yedidyah Herrero is the author of *Colonial Jukebox: Poems* (KC Press). A native of Florida, he teaches college courses in Caribbean literature, most recently in New York and San Francisco.

What You Keep

SUZANNE HICKS

When you were little you wanted to be a movie star and told your grandma when you visited that you had to use Camay soap because that's what movie stars used, so she bought you the little bars of the soap, imprinted with the silhouette of a lady you thought looked glamorous just like Judy Garland who starred in your favorite movie and sang "Somewhere Over the Rainbow" so beautifully, you wanted to sound just like her when you sang the song for your grandma who left a house full of years and years of clutter and treasures when she died, and when everyone was rummaging through her things, staking their claim to the tea cups, jewelry, paintings, even the coveted green lamp, you found an old bar of Camay soap hidden in the back of the linen closet among expired medications, old bandages, and musty smelling sheets, that you tucked in your pocket before you went to get some fresh air in the backyard and look at the tulips that you helped your grandma plant in the garden because all you ever wanted from her was already yours.

Reservoir

SUZANNE HICKS

*A man was found with a beating heart at the busy inter-
section of Las Vegas Boulevard and Tropicana Avenue
on Tuesday. Authorities arrived on the scene at quite an
ordinary time of day and found the man shouting, I'm
alive! I'm alive! The man was taken to the hospital, where
he was determined to be very much alive and well. The
situation is being investigated as highly suspicious.*

*A little white wedding chapel on Las Vegas Boulevard
announced Wednesday it would be ceasing all wedding
ceremonies and will be exclusively providing drive-through
break-up services. All severances of relationships will be
performed, including ending short and long-term non-
binding relationships, common law marriages, and annul-
ments. The concept has received widespread community
support, and the chapel expects there to be a long line of
couples on the first day of the new operation who wish to
terminate their relationships in a positive manner to honor
the time they shared.*

*On Thursday, the local water authority announced that
Lake Mead's water level is predicted to rise significantly
due to the high precipitation over the winter. The generous*

snowpack in the Rockies is much-needed good news for the drought-stricken region.

When the temperature rises, and the snow begins to melt and trickle down to the martini glass-shaped reservoir, people flock to the lake with their boats hinged to their trucks, but instead of launching them into the water, they circle the bank, finding the best views, climbing up onto the roof of their trucks, hanging off the tailgates, lounging under the canopies of their boats, and the people hold hands with their former lovers and strangers who will become their lovers as everyone stares at the water, eyes fixed on the bathtub ring, some saying they've never seen the lake so blue, some saying they can see the rise, while the man who was found with a beating heart at the busy intersection of Las Vegas Boulevard and Tropicana Avenue wanders among them whispering, *We're alive! We're alive!*

Suzanne Hicks is a disabled writer living with multiple sclerosis. Her stories have appeared in *Gone Lawn*, *Milk Candy Review*, *Atlas and Alice*, *Maudlin House*, *Roi Fainéant Press*, *New Flash Fiction Review*, and elsewhere. Read more at suzannehickswrites.com

Spinning

JUDE HIGGINS

After her husband left, she thought it would be good for her emotional well-being to keep in regular contact with friends and family. People who cared. Today, she'd rung Daisy, her daughter, several times but she hadn't answered. A conversation with her, or anyone would be so welcome. Had no-one remembered it was one year, six weeks and two days since she'd been alone after thirty years of marriage?

To make her mobile ring, she spun her silver cake knives in circles, once every hour. If someone rang and the call lasted two minutes, she would allow herself a cinnamon bun. On the fourth hour, the phone rang. Not her daughter, but Marco, a pleasant sounding young man from Sunlit Futures. She kept him talking. Yes, she was interested in green energy, yes, she would buy solar panels. She asked him about his working conditions, if many people put the phone down on him as soon as he spoke?

'Yes, people frequently do that,' he said, his voice reassuring. 'And it's lovely for a change, to speak to someone who appreciates the importance of renewable energy.'

'It's lovely to think that energy can be renewed,' she said, remembering whirling around the ballroom floor in her dancing days, when her husband still loved her.

But after she told Marco she couldn't give him her bank details and didn't want a stranger coming round to measure up — her daughter told her never to agree to such things — he said he had to go.

'I'll still consider all your offers,' she added, hastily. 'Can you phone again?'

'Of course,' he said, kindly. 'What about tomorrow?'

Six minutes had elapsed during the call, so she ate three cinnamon buns to celebrate, then rang her daughter, on repeat, to tell her the good news.

Jude Higgins' flash fictions have been widely published in magazines and anthologies. Her chapbook, *The Chemist's House*, was published by V. Press in 2017. She runs Bath Flash Fiction Award and directs the short fiction press Ad Hoc Fiction and Flash Fiction Festivals, UK.

One Fell Off

KEITH HOOD

I would have never thought of the idea on my own. My wife was the one who worked in white people's homes. She was the one who'd said, "They put these marks on a door frame to count they children's height. I tried washing them marks off first time I saw 'em, but that white woman said, 'What the hell you think you're doing, girl?'" She didn't say n*****, but Amelia knew that was how the sentence ended in the woman's mind. So I started drawing the measuring lines on our kitchen door frame with Rochelle, our last born. She was two years old when I started counting her height. She wasn't the last person to die in the 1967 riot. The last person was number thirty-nine. Rochelle was number fifteen. When her world ended, she was barely three years old. I couldn't count past that.

I could count backwards, like in childhood rhymes we shared: "There was ten in bed and the little one said, 'roll over,'" or "Five little monkeys jumpin' on the bed. One fell off and bumped his head." Ten in bed, so they all rolled over, one fell out, nine in bed. Five monkeys in bed to four. Rochelle fell while sleeping on her bed, bullet through head, blood on pillow and sheets. Two left over—firstborn Ronnie and secondborn Regina—and I'm living "Ninety-Nine Bottles of Beer on the Wall" with twelve-packs of E & B.

Keith Hood is a former janitor and window cleaner from Michigan. He retired from a job as a field technician for a Michigan electric utility after 32 years avoiding electrocution. Keith is the 2024 *One Story* magazine Adina Talve-Goodman Fellow. His work has appeared in eighteen journals.

The Punch

Tiffany Hsieh

I shot the puck but it hit the goalie. That was Tuesday. The next day the moron looked like this pug-faced avatar I killed fifty-seven times in a video game. That was back in spring break, senior year. That week everybody I knew went upstate and I went downstairs. Ma pegged socks and underwear on a clothesline tied to a water pipe that gurgled every time Ba flushed the toilet upstairs, in the bathroom next to the guest room that was once Bro's. Bro was the best goalie on the block when we were kids. He wore his mask like a pro, sure as hell never took it off in front of the net, and beat up anyone who tripped me. Billy, now a sales associate at Toyota. Jackson, dumb enough to knock up a girl from NorCal and follow her to Canada. Liam, in prison for something no one seemed to know much about. Bro didn't like these guys but he liked them enough to buy a used Corolla from Billy, drive to Toronto for Jackson's shotgun, visit Liam's parents whenever he was home. Like Christmas and Lunar New Year. I used to think I should stop by too, see about getting some info on Sally, Liam's sister. We hung out a few times. Popcorn, movies, parking lots. The last time, in the backseat of her parents' Oldsmobile, she swirled her tongue in my mouth and said I was not bad for a dork. Later, around the time I joined the men's league, I realized girls called you a dork when they liked you but wished you weren't actually so dorky. Sally was the smart one. She got into Yale and never texted. Not even emojis. I was just some dork who made her horny once and I was fine with that. I went out for a beer on Friday. The goalie from Tuesday was there with his broken nose and a knuckled fist. It came out of nowhere and fast and I saw stars, real ones. I think I even tasted Sally's bubble gum too. Leathery, a hint of strawberry, very masticated.

Tiffany Hsieh is the author of the poetry collection *Pork Fluff* (forthcoming from Sundress Publications) and the micro chapbook *Little Red* (Quarter Press). She lives in Kingston, Ontario.

Ghost Story

MATTHEW JAKUBOWSKI

Ghost with a gun. Ghost in the desert. Ghost wearing a cool hat.

Ghost who can phase through the earth but prefers to walk. Ghost who wears a white sheet sometimes, and sometimes has shadowy feet, which sometimes make a slight noise, just for fun. Ghost with a good sense of humor that's lost on almost everyone.

Ghost with a new gun. Stolen! Ghost who can drink you under the table. Old ghost in the wild west who suddenly shows up in a Honda Fit and is like hey oh sorry I time-traveled I can do that. 'Bye! Ghost who comes back to town later riding a buffalo and pretends none of that car stuff happened.

Ghost sitting out in the open eating stolen food it can't even digest or taste but who hangs out all day at the food court ruining the food with ectoplasm and when a teenager finally gets up the courage to yell at it the ghost says, "Good-bye, cruel world!" and crawls away very slowly into a video arcade.

Ghost having a bad day. Ghost wearing the jersey of that team everybody hates. Ghost with a shoe on its head. Ghost watching Ghostbusters and crying.

Ghost clearing its head getting away from it all, riding a horse, and the horse is pretty freaked out but later, after the ghost sets it free, it dreams of an island in Montana where wild horses used to thrive and actually makes it there, but dies the same day.

Ghost sitting at a bar in Bozeman with a few serious drunkards who are laughing and yell to the other scared patrons and ghost tourists, "See! We told you. But no, you said. Shut up, you said."

Ghost who used to pop up out of the ground in the middle of showdowns and shout la-la-la and dance in a circle right when the duelers drew their pistols just to get a laugh out of its buddy death.

Tired ghost. Ghost of my heart. Ghost of my old self. Ghost of my old selves' hearts. Ghosts who got lucky. Ghost who will probably be fine. Ghost of the woods and the rivers and good carpets and perfect coffee. Ghost of good luck. Ghost we hope to have, to help us cross over when it's time.

Matthew Jakubowski (mattjakubowski.com) is a rather tall writer from Virginia. He's lived in West Philadelphia for 15 years and goes to the park a lot to read or write or ride a skateboard. When there's Shakespeare in the park or jazz, he'll be out there. West Philly is amazing.

A Wednesday in Dhaka

Pooja Joshi

The driver tells me the air conditioning has been acting up. *Fuck.* I sit back against the leather seat, praying that my makeup remains intact. I can already feel a rivulet of sweat mixed with foundation running down the side of my face. We haven't moved in fifteen minutes. That's five o'clock on a Wednesday in Dhaka for you. I push the buds of my headphones deeper into my ears, but the noise canceling function is futile against the relentless cacophony of honking that surrounds us.

There's a tap on my window. It's a girl – can't be more than ten or twelve – selling flowers. I grimace, averting my eyes from the pane of glass. I don't have anything less than a five hundred taka note on me. If I had a ten or twenty on me, I would've bought a flower. At least that's what I tell myself. She puts her nose against the glass, her stare boring into my soul. It's as if she knows what I'm thinking and judges me for it. Me, the one sitting in a car complaining about air conditioning, who routinely buys mediocre coffee that I promptly forget to finish for five hundred taka. But for her? That same note would mean she could go home. The cracked skin on her feet would get some rest. If she ran fast enough, she could sneak into the back bench at school and still satisfy her parents with her earnings for the day.

My cheeks feel hot. I can't tell if it's from me thinking about what she's thinking about me or if it's just because the air conditioning isn't working. Fuck it. I dig into my purse and pull out the green bill. Her face breaks out into a wide smile as I roll down the window and hand it to her. She tries to give me all her flowers but I shake my head and just pick one. *Bhalo thaken*, I say to her. *Stay well.* She laughs at my accent and bows, before scampering off across six lanes of traffic.

Pooja Joshi is a Desi writer from North Carolina. She is currently based in Boston, where she is pursuing an MBA and MPP at Harvard University. Previously, she has worked in health tech strategy and management consulting. Her work has been published in *The Ilanot Review*, *The Hooghly Review*, and in a short story collection from Atomic Carnival Books, among others.

When the Cowbirds Come to Carry Your Sister Away

Audra Kerr Brown

They descend in clattering droves, sag telephone lines, drip from the tulip tree like rotten fruit. You watch from the window, push your nose against the pane. Your mother tells you about a sudden spring snow-storm, about a speckled egg found on the doorstep. How she candled the shell and saw a sleeping girl tucked inside. Saw the shiver of her mustard seed heart. How she knew this day would come.

When the cowbirds come to carry your sister away, it all makes sense to you now: your sister's penchant for heights, her constant preening, the way she greets each day with a song. Your mother buckles your sister's shoes, smooths the stubborn wings of her Peter Pan collar. Kisses the top of her head as she sends her out the door: *What a pretty girl, such a pretty girl.* Your sister looks back at your mother, blinks her bead black eyes.

When the cowbirds come to carry your sister away, they hook her in a tangle of claw and beak, swallow her in a cloud of beating feathers, then disappear—

a tight fist into the gloaming. You rip the curtains, tear the sashes. You cry for your cowbird sister until your mother claps her hands, shushes you quiet. It's then you catch your reflection in the darkened glass— the press of pointed teeth against your lower lip, the twitch of ears when your mother pats the sofa: *Be a good boy, come sit.*

Audra Kerr Brown's work has appeared in the *Best Small Fictions* and *Wigleaf*'s Top 50 Very Short Fictions List. She is the founding creator of the (sometimes) YouTube channel, *The Flashtronauts!* which explores the "ever-expanding universe of Flash Fiction." Her chapbook, *hush hush hush*, is available at Harbor Editions.

The Angel Gabriel Says It's Not a Booty Call if He Doesn't Have Genitals,

FRANCES KLEIN

And he doesn't. He comes over at three am, pulls down his joggers and shows me what he calls "the light of pure goodness." The light seems mediocre at best, but I go along with it. The Angel Gabriel wants intimacy in these smallest hours of the morning, so we compare embarrassing adolescent photos, me with my self-cut baby bangs, him with his infinite number of eyes. He lies on my bed, head hanging over the edge, legs stretched up against the wall. We kiss once, as the sunrise checks its watch on the other side of the horizon, but The Angel Gabriel doesn't know how. He pulls his lips all the way back, meets mine with his perfectly straight, dry teeth. We lie side by side on the bed, and I fall asleep somewhere in the middle of The Angel Gabriel telling me which US Presidents are in hell, which is all of them. In the morning, the pillow still holds the indent of his head.

Frances Klein is an Alaskan poet and teacher. Klein is the author of several poetry chapbooks, including *(Text) Messages from The*

Angel Gabriel (2024). Her full-length collection *Another Life* is forthcoming in 2025. Klein's writing has appeared in *The Harvard Advocate*, *The Atticus Review*, *HAD*, and others.

Genie

KIP KNOTT

The last time I saw my father, he was a gray cloud of ashes drifting over the rail of the Sunday Creek Bridge. At first he fell to pieces the way he used to do after mom died when the chaos of three kids pulled him in all directions and he gathered himself in the bottom of a bottle like a genie in reverse, leaving his hungry children's wishes unfulfilled. But then he coalesced into something more than the fragments of what he had become and something less than who he had been, a man who chose to drown himself, along with his children, in self-pity and 7-and-7s. He hovered for a moment over the slivered surface of the drought-battered river. His mouth formed a kind of snarl as his whiskey-ravaged voice whispered words only the wind could hear. I waved my arms—not in surrender, but to scatter him into nothingness. And when he finally fell all the way down into the rocky river, I prayed that what little water was left would be enough to carry him far away from me. Just to be sure as I screwed the lid of his urn tight, I muttered, "I wish for rain," and dropped it down among the rocks so I could never open that bottle again.

Kip Knott is a writer, teacher, photographer, and part-time art dealer living in Delaware, Ohio. He spends his spare time traveling the back roads of Appalachia and the Midwest taking photographs and searching for lost art treasures.

Sibling Parenting

SHIH-LI KOW

Ai Ping's brother said women who habitually declared they found happiness in everyday things were the hardest to please. If a woman required x affirmations of happiness a day, each having an effect which lasted an average y minutes, then she must, in fact, default to a state of misery $(1\text{-}xy)$ of the time. His algebra was explained in a growing-up talk when Ai Ping reached puberty. It was a matter of frequency and duration, he said, and for a moment, she thought he meant her period. She was twelve. She wanted her cramps to go away and her breasts to grow.

When he said he was engaged, she thought he was joking, but he wasn't. Ai Ping asked if he loved her, this friend/girlfriend now fiancée. It seemed like a grown-up thing to ask, with a little frown of concern, "But do you love her?" He said, "Enough to marry her. There's plenty of time to work on it after." And Ai Ping thought of love as a slow thing formed with time, the x's and y's expanding within the embrace of the parentheses like a plant in a bottle garden.

When his fiancée left him, her brother thought it

was a prank, but it wasn't. An ungrateful woman who expected too much was a doomed, ravenous creature, he blustered. A princess-witch who wanted the big rescue, the fairy tale, and perfectly timed doses of small and shiny pleasures. He said Ai Ping would do well to decide which to give up—the prince, the godmother, or the golden goose—before she started believing she could have them all.

Ai Ping was fourteen now, old enough to know that he was bitter and full of crap. The more she thought about his $(1-xy)$, the less sense it made. If only he'd stop bellyaching about how right he was, she'd tell him that a frog who spouted a bit of math was still a frog, and a girl could be an equation all by herself with just two X's and no Y's. She'd tell him alright. He'd do well to listen.

Shih-Li Kow is the author of two short story collections and a novel. Her latest book, *Bone Weight and Other Stories*, is a cross-genre collection of twenty-five stories. She lives in Kuala Lumpur, Malaysia.

Past Imperfect

LOUELLA LESTER

LOPSIDED

Mom was wrapping, tucking, and pulling the shoelace, demonstrating a perfect bow. "Now, you do the other foot."

WOBBLED

Dad was visiting, his long fingers going almost all the way around the football, touching the laces that face away, throwing a perfect spiral. "You give it a try."

BROKEN

My best friend was punching the pocket of her brother's old baseball glove, telling me to watch so I can imitate her, then examining the laces, and perfectly catching the ball. "Okay, now I'll throw to you."

TORN

My older sister was lending me her favourite dress, helping me into it, the ribbon lacing up to perfectly cinch at the back. "Don't try to undo it yourself or let some stupid boy at it, eh?"

RIPPED

The guy at the bar was pulling a tiny pipe from his pocket, smiling with his perfect teeth, hooking his fingers into the laces fronting his jeans. "Can you help me with this?"

DAMAGED

He was lying on a lumpy mattress on the floor, eyes perfectly glazed, saying, "Honey, there's no choice, we need the money," while smoking the last of something laced with something else.

Louella Lester is a writer/photographer in Winnipeg, Canada, author of *Glass Bricks* (At Bay Press), and a contributing editor at *NFFR*. Her writing has appeared recently in *Gooseberry Pie*, *Bright Flash*, *SoFloPoJo*, *The Ekphrastic Review*, *Cult. Magazine*, *The Dribble Drabble Review*, *MacQueen's Quinterly*, and a variety of other journals.

Mother Tongue

Kik Lodge

On the train, a girl licks the window and her mother tells her to stop licking the window, but the girl carries on, and there's me thinking let her lick the window, the cold must feel nice on her tongue, she's licking the trees through the glass, the buildings, the schools, the cyclists, let her lick, she's licking the traffic lights, the potholed people, the cows, and her mother yanks her by the hood and the girl's zip digs into her throat as she falls back, squashed against the buggy with a baby in it, stay put the mother says, and I say but she wasn't doing any harm, let her lick the fucking window, and the mother says something mean and another passenger says something which is probably to back her up because they're both looking at me and then another passenger starts shaking his head and there's the storm in my ears again, a thousand thunders, and I'm back in the damp shed and the door is locked from the outside and you have to seriously think, I mean seriously think, about what you have done if you want to come back in the house, and through the slits sits the moon and the moon is all mine and when I reach with my tongue I can taste it.

Kik Lodge is a short fiction writer from Devon, England, but she lives in Lyon, France, with a menagerie of kids and cats. When she is not writing, she is not cooking or running either. Her flash collection *Scream If You Want To* is out with Alien Buddha Press. Erratic tweets @KikLodge

U.S. Threat Forecast

Andrea Marcusa

Did you know that frogs grow noisy before it rains? And dogs and cats always sense tornadoes looming. Also, wind is silent; we only hear it when it blows against something. Even though little can be learned about people from their facial features, our noses can detect a trillion smells. Meteorologists say lightning strikes 20 million times a year but kills only 432. And hailstones can grow as large as baseballs. 316 people are shot daily and 48,222 die each year from gunshot wounds. Bullets from an AR-15 travel almost three times faster than one from a handgun and liquefy organs, leaving a smashed cavity the size of a grapefruit. Although wives' tales say otherwise, lightning often hits in the same location twice, sometimes more. And cats really do land on their feet. It takes blood 60 seconds to make a complete circuit of the body. Scientists tell us that full moons don't impact human behavior, but violence rates rise along with air temperature. A simple way to learn the air temperature is to count the number of cricket chirps in 15 seconds and add 40. One definition of the word *execution* is "to carry out a plan." Blood tastes as salty as an ocean. In time, people grow accustomed to violence, especially young children. Did you know that the only muscle that never tires out in the human body is the beating heart? And sound, whether the blast of a gun or tinkle of a baby's laugh, won't ever carry in the absolute silence of outer space. Psychologists say it's normal to feel upset following a distressing news event, but the feeling eases after a few weeks as predictably as snow melting each spring.

Andrea Marcusa's work has appeared in the *Gettysburg Review*, *Cutbank*, *River Teeth*, *Citron Review*, *Milk Candy Review* and others. She's received recognition in a range of competitions, including *SmokeLong*, *Best Microfiction*, *Cleaver* and others. She lives in New York City where she is a member of the faculty of The Writers Studio and studies with poet Philip Schultz.

Past Jack Koo's shop
A faux pantoum

FRANKIE MCMILLAN

We kids were drawn to the backs of things. Back of Jack Koo's shop, wooden crates of rotten bananas, clouds of tiny flies. Back of Solly's car yards, wrecked parts, oil sumps, then to the backyard of the richest family in the street. We heard music, Frank Sinatra floating over the fence. We peered through a hole in the fence. In the yard a man was shaving a woman's underarms. We kids started pushing and shoving to get a better look. We heard the man shout and we ran. But after a while, we were drawn back. Back to the fence hole.

The woman wore a red bandana, face tilted to the sun, arms raised behind her head. He was shaving her underarms. We didn't know if this was love. We kept going back to the fence hole. Frank Sinatra singing ... *five foot two, eyes of blue* ... They were the richest family in the street. Same street as Jack Koo's shop, wooden crates of rotten bananas, clouds of tiny flies. We heard the man shout. He heard us pushing and shoving at the fence hole. He looked up, stared around the yard. Razor flashing. She wore a red bandana, face tilted to the sun, arms raised behind her head. He was shaving her underarms. He was shaving her. This was past Jack Koo's shop. We didn't know if this was love.

Frankie McMillan is a poet and short fiction writer from Aotearoa, New Zealand. Her latest book, *The Wandering Nature of Us Girls* (Canterbury University Press), was published in 2022.

Method for a Sunday Roast

SIAN MEADES-WILLIAMS

I didn't know, then, to drizzle carrots with honey. To glaze them with sweetness until my teeth squeaked and my shoulders relaxed into the rest of my body. I had no idea the patience needed for a potato to crisp around the edges without losing its softness. Or that red cabbage is most deserving of affection from nutmeg and cinnamon. Tenderness is not my area of expertise, but I've learnt that without it, dryness will choke the life out of you. A thin gravy cannot save that. No matter how much floods your plate, stopping just short of the rim, it will still be lacking. So add to it the very bones of a life. Make it thick with richness. After all of the mistakes, failed attempts, tweaks, this feels like the backbone of my kitchen. My mainstay. Hundreds of Sundays passed before I realised how liberally I could season my life. The salt was always there, in the blue ceramic bowl, ready for me to grab by the fistful.

Sian Meades-Williams is an author and poet living in London. Her recent poetry has been published by *Green Ink Poetry* and *little living room*. She is the author of several non-fiction books, and her historical novel-in-progress, *Belville*, won the 2022 Yeovil Literary Prize.

A tiny, tiny bit of beauty

LAILA MILLER

The water by now has lost its mud, settled into a greenish gloom that every so often burps up a consumable: a cushion embroidered gold with peacocks, an empty plant pot, a toothbrush; and it's like holiday traffic on the single lane to Hamilton, blurry and red and loud with Ed Sheeran at first, then slow, stopped in a glug, then grunting forward and you eventually see why, and don't want to look, but can't help but look and you stop the track and wonder if that toothbrush belonged to someone you knew and where were they now and could they get a new one because it was something you needed every day and you wouldn't purposely lose it or let a monster swallow it, and if you rolled down your car window, held your breath and let the rain in, your toothbrush would be the last thing you let float away even if you were going fast, which you weren't because time had slowed, then poured its contents out onto the lawn and the street and would you ever get it all back and maybe you shouldn't think about it in case the car ahead has lost more than you. The Sun's out now, finally, finally, and you blink at the glistening shards of glass, the sparkling waves, and it's a tiny, tiny bit of beauty.

Laila Miller writes short fiction about bougainvilleas and sea urchins and turnips, and sometimes about people who don't get along. Her work can be found in *Flash Frontier*, *Hippocampus*, *Cricket Magazine*, and elsewhere. Originally from Canada, she lives in Perth, Western Australia, with her husband and son.

Culloden

Dawn Miller

In my memory, black-clothed strangers shuffle by my brother's open casket while above, a yellow and orange banner of number 8 hockey sweaters shouts from corner to corner and my mother hunkers, smaller now, more bitter, yet watchful, the note she wrote in spidery script *Don't Touch Sean* propped against the coffin's white satin interior—and still, in my memory, my father sits beside her and hasn't left to wander across Delancey Street to Kelly's Grill—*a genius place for a bar*, Dad says—to toss back rye and Coke, planting his foot on the first rung of the ladder he'll climb until he later dies, yellow-eyed and liver football-hard—and in another moment, amongst the cloying tang of blood-red roses, Grandma Jessie grabs my twelve-year-old hand like an anchor and whispers in her gentle Nova Scotian lilt *God chooses to call the best home—that's why our Sean did what he did*—and bagpipes heave and weep in the background, heave and weep like the sorrow of Culloden battlefields where last summer Sean and I wandered from the tourist museum under the gun-metal sky and sprinted over slick, dewy hills to spy a kilted woman with flowing red locks pour a dram of whiskey on each grass-covered mound and Sean said *I want to be a hero when I grow up*—and then later still, my father plays the same highland melody on the stereo in a repeated loop, the volume set loud but not loud enough to mask my mother's keening while I lie in bed across from Sean's darkened room, pillows pressed tight to my ears, and shout *turn it down, turn it all down.*

Dawn Miller's work appears or is forthcoming in *The Cincinnati Review*, *The Forge Literary Magazine*, *SmokeLong Quarterly*, *Fractured Lit*, *Atticus Review*, *Room Magazine*, and elsewhere. She lives and writes in Picton, Ontario, Canada.

In Case of Emergency

Erin Murphy

Where would we live if you and Daddy died? our daughter asks at dinner. Our teenage son looks up from his spaghetti-spooled fork, interested, for once, in something his younger sister has said. We are not planning to die anytime soon. But our daughter is good at questions. When she was two, she asked if a knife could cut another knife. At first, a digression: our son mentions foster care, wonders aloud if they'd have to change schools. Then my daughter says, *Yeah, and we'd have to take a special bus with the other kids of parents who died.* We run with this idea. *The Orphan Bus! It would be black! It would drive with its lights on all day like a hearse! All the other cars would pull over to let it pass!* But it's sweet, really, the thought that her loss would be so all-consuming that she'd have to segregate herself, unable even to engage in normal school bus banter. It occurs to me that she has barely been brushed by death. Even Romeo, her betta fish, has outlived our expectations. Back to the original question: *If Daddy and I died*, I say, *Grandma and Grandpa would come to live with you. You wouldn't have to change houses or schools.* This is not something I have discussed with my mother and stepfather, but I feel certain they'd rise to the occasion. I watch my children roll this idea around in their minds. *Okay, so our parents are dead, but we get to keep the same bedrooms, the same friends, the same lockers at school,* they seem to be thinking. *But what if they die?* our daughter wants to know. I offer surrogate B. *And if she dies?* Surrogate C. *And if she dies?* I am quickly exhausting the list of people who would be willing, on a moment's notice, to drop their own lives, move to central/western Pennsylvania, and raise my kids. And here our son— who has already flirted with transformation, who finds hair sprouting in unexpected places, who sees his former Little League teammates toking joints behind the YMCA, who once watched a video of himself as a young boy and said, *Man, this me would hate that me*—here our son interrupts. *If she died,* he says, *we'd both be arrested for murder 'cause everyone who lives with us ends up dead.* And he is right—not that he and his sister would be arrested, but that we should end this conversation, and we should end it laughing.

Erin Murphy is author or editor of thirteen books of poetry and prose. Her work has appeared in *The Best of Brevity*, *Ecotone*, *Waxwing*, *Guesthouse*, *Rattle*, *Women's Studies Quarterly*, and elsewhere. She is professor of English at Penn State Altoona. www.erin-murphy.com

College Boy and the County Fair

CHRISTOPHER NOTARNICOLA

Auntie was cutting vegetables like they weren't even there, asking why I was worried about who would ride the Ferris Wheel with whom when these girls out here—hacking the back end of a butcher knife through the side of a sweet onion—were always wearing some too-tight torn-up see-through something over popped-up nipples like it's cool to be cold. She stabbed a peel and brought the handle to her breast. Oh, she said with a moan, twirling the blade. I told her she'd better stop, swallowing a smile. Onion sting filled the air. She returned to the cutting board and told me I should hang out on campus instead of around the old neighborhood, get in with the ones who stay through spring semester, drink coffee, quote a poet, find a woman with clothes over her chest, a woman I could bring home for dinner, with appetite, whip smart but kind, a wholesome woman. The stockpot was steaming on the stove. Double Jeopardy was starting by the microwave. Alex Trebek was dead, and the soup was already reminding me of my mother. The word wholesome, I said, is composed of opposites—isn't that funny. Auntie paused her dice, hovering over half-moons of onion, knuckles at the wide edge of the blade, tears jeweling the ends of her lashes, and she looked to the TV, maybe wondering if I had stolen the line from a category or if I had brought that one to the table on my own. The camera panned, and the contestants were at their buzzers. Boy, she said, if you don't start peeling carrots.

Christopher Notarnicola's work has appeared in *AGNI*, *American Short Fiction*, *Bellevue Literary Review*, *Best American Essays*, *Chicago Quarterly Review*, *Image*, *River Teeth*, *The Southampton Review* and other publications. Find him in Fort Lauderdale, Florida, and at christophernotarnicola.com

9/11 in Owensboro, Kentucky

Thomas O'Connell

Everyone sat around their living rooms watching television. 24-hour newsfeeds. Updates that actually told us nothing. We all believed that our miniature town would be a potential target. We all silently imagined an airplane flying into the twelve-story hotel downtown. While floating in the swimming pool, I watched a plane fly overhead. It felt like the most familiar thing in the world. It felt like nothing I had ever experienced before.

A librarian living by the banks of the Connecticut River in Springfield, Massachusetts, Thomas O'Connell has published poetry and short fiction in *Jellyfish Review*, *Blink-Ink*, *Your Impossible Voice*, *Live Nude Poems*, *Hobart*, and *The Los Angeles Review*, as well as other print and online journals.

Spin Cycle

JUDITH OSILÉ OHIKUARE

—Like the laundry: I really couldn't get a grip on that last load. I had decided to dump everything in all at once (there was so much and I had so little time), so in went EJ's basketball uniforms and my de-elasticized bras and Dana's period panties and Elijah's boxer briefs. The washer cycled while I checked things off my to-do list for an hour (emails, bills, defrosting meat), but when I returned to take everything out, I found myself pulling and pulling—I mean seriously going at it with the machine—for ages. I was nearly diving in at one point.

The clothes hadn't fully spun dry, so I was soaked and cold, but I stood there, *yanking*, and finding more than I'd actually put in. Things I thought I'd lost forever, like my favorite socks to wear to bed and a thong bodysuit I hated that pinched the rind of skin between my ass cheeks. I found a shirt my dad used to wear while working on his car and a funeral shroud the color of sandalwood that was rough and sopping. I had no idea whose it was and didn't want to know yet.

After two more hours of this, the very last items I tugged free were the clothes I had been wearing at the start. I looked down at myself, shivering, to realize I had nothing on but my house shoes and a satin bonnet. The dryer was running and I could hear the garbage men pulling away from the curb. The reek of spoiled castoffs filtered in through the vent.

Upstairs, the kids argued over who would toast their Pop-Tarts first, until I remembered that I had no house and no kids and no husband—only a two-year lease that was set to expire on my birthday and an upcoming date with Elijah I'd been ambivalent about for weeks. He wanted to surprise me, but I don't like not knowing what to wear.

Judith Osilé Ohikuare is a poet, fiction writer, and former journalist. She has performed at Lincoln Center's "Poets on the Plaza" and is a 2023-2024 Fellow for In Surreal Life. Her work has been published in HAD, Variant Literature, hex, CHEAP POP, and anthologized in Best Microfiction 2023.

In Leaping

MANDIRA PATTNAIK

Sometimes, standing before the mirror, Leia would say she felt like a grasshopper. Say this to herself while the toddlers slept.

Unlike the meadows back home, her floor is ash-ridden, and her antenna reaches out to the neighbor's window, but they can't see or hear her. If they cared to ask, if ever, Leia would say she leaves behind children, too hungry, too clipped to find out what she does, disappearing every morning, before daybreak, and if she brings them food, the windows make a rattling sound because the kids shout in such joy.

I know, she says softly, on the night before Sunday, and disconnects the call from a distant relative in a faraway land; the harvest done, so her people have made a little money to put through a call to her, and say they are worried about her. Ask, when she'll come back, though secretly they hope she never does, they can't afford more mouths.

Leia wraps her hands over her thin grasshopper legs, she can't sleep, remains in sitting position all through the night, feels hungry, thinks if she had ears in the abdomen, like a grasshopper's, would they turn deaf because her stomach's always grumbling? Maybe it'll take stronger springs in her hind legs to catapult her, more distorted thinking, to forget Sundays are weekly paydays, and the night before is when all provisions are exhausted. It'll take still longer to finally fly.

Sometimes, in leaping, endlessly, she forgets she has wings.

Mandira Pattnaik is the author of four chapbooks. Her work has appeared in *Penn Review, McNeese Review, AAWW, Contrary, The Rumpus* and others. Visit her at mandirapattnaik.com

Contortionists

KEITH J. POWELL

Mom survived on backbenders, splits, torques, and twists. *Don't avoid the truth,* she said. *Avoid bumping into the lie.* She collected dodges the way others plucked coins from sidewalks, pocketing them to buy her way out of trouble later. Always limber and prepared, Mom's pretzeled confabulations inevitably dazzled her inquisitors, defusing their heated accusations. I wish I'd studied her act more closely. Years later, when a stray motel receipt exposed my intimate tumblings, I had no ready excuse. I was left sputtering, stiff and graceless before my wounded husband, my heart beating like clapping hands, urging the show to begin.

Keith J. Powell is co-founder of *Your Impossible Voice*. Find more of his writing at www.keithjpowell.com and @keithjpowell. bsky.social

Beautification

KEN POYNER

The boy is dressed in a day-suit. Short little knickers that cut below the knees when he stands, but which ride up above his knees when he sits. His white socks grow only to the ankles, leaving a stretch of his leg to view when he stands, more leg and the knee itself when he sits. His shoes are made of that fake patent leather that never needs polish, but which over time cracks and in one failing comes completely undone. They have a single strap across the top of each and would be as appropriate for a young girl as for a young boy. He has to reach up to hold his father's hand. As they wait, he twists side to side and when his father is aware of the twisting, he tugs the boy's hand. The boy stops until he senses his father's attention has moved on, and then he begins his twisting again, small at first, but growing until the father must notice. I place five dollars on the boy. He is up next. I have nothing on the current match, but one boy in the ring is crying as the other boy bites into his upper arm. In pain, the first boy forgets to parry and retreat, kick and advance. It is difficult to keep focus at his age when in pain, but the boy

I've bet on for the next match seems to know how to test limits, to dismiss the hard meanings of things, to push his luck.

Proof

Ken Poyner

To be a successful clownherd, he needs to understand the why of clowns. The drive and sway, the mathematics, the mechanics of clowns. His plan is to slowly introduce himself secretly into the herd. He will put on his yellow multi-tier stove-pipe hat, his water-shooting daisy, the purple tie and outsized pavement slapping shoes, spend a day frolicking with them. He will then slip out as translucently as he wedged in, summing his experience at length with the experiences of others, comparing it with the master clown encyclopedia. With his collected data digested and his expectations refined, he will re-engage the collective, masked as a different, more precise clown. Each infiltration will stretch longer and cover more eddies of the herd until he understands the arc of clowndom, the curing of clowndom, the maturity of the profile. Take care, failed clownherds practicing before him have warned: learn all that you can but hold a sliver of stoic academic distance. Clownery can become native. If it grabs you, you cannot be the clownherd: you join the herd. You become the clown. And then everything makes the wrong sense.

Ken Poyner's nine books of poetry, flash, and micro-fiction are available at a few bookstores, and online at Amazon, B&N, and elsewhere. Retired from 33 years as a computer specialist, he now cheers for his world-class powerlifting wife of 46+ years at her various contests.

The Contortionist

IMOGEN RAE

After every show, when the crowds shuffle home with the stage lights still winking in their eyes and buttery popcorn kernels refusing to digest in their stomachs, you crawl into your trailer, the one where the freaks sleep. In the corner, on a vinyl table, is your jar. It's transparent glass, glinting and round, as tall as your torso. The sort of jar that, in another world, might store candies or biscuits on somebody's mother's kitchen counter, but this one is just big enough for you.

On stage, you are hot all the time. You wear almost nothing, but the lights and eyes are scalding. During your routine, you stuff yourself into a suitcase to be carried, when you unfold you become arachnid. You crawl about with your feet flung over your head, moving on fingers and toes, neck craned painfully upwards to leer at the audience who leer back. Afterwards, you languish in the spotlight, stretching and stretching, twisting until you feel like you could tear, and you could. You know the audience is confused during your act. You dance between repulsive and arousing, showing them everything they thought they wanted to see. You become queasy with shame, feel your eyes turning plastic and rolling up into your head.

While the trailer is still empty you pull the lid off of that cool, glass jar and step inside. Your joints pop and your skin stretches, the ache of it familiar and soft through your tired muscles. There is only one comfortable position for sleeping here. Every limb must be wrapped close around you, feet up, hands down. Flatten and shrink. You hold your head at a sharp angle and press your open face against the glass and when it's all done and your breath is blooming like the wings of birds, you feel as if you are in the womb. Cradled, shoulders dislocated. Your feet twisted tightly around your bent neck, a little choking, a little like a lover.

Imogen Rae lives, works, and studies in Cheltenham, England. She loves animals and writing short fiction. Her work has appeared in *New Flash Fiction Review* and was shortlisted for the *WestWord* Prize 2023.

Yarnidermis

RUBY RORTY

There is a woman made of yarn and all day she sits and knits. She has already knitted herself and her home and her daughter so now she knits sweaters. It is a good thing the yarn woman runs cold because she is, right now as I write this, wearing ten sweaters and knitting an eleventh. The overall impression is that of a furry, multicolored person with extremely thick skin around their arms and torso: yarnidermis is what I would call it if I were a scientist.

The yarn woman is my grandmother but I am not made of yarn. Being made of yarn is a recessive trait. Inside my grandmother, yarn twists in double helices and spools in nuclei. Scientists are always trying to untangle my grandmother. We keep spray bottles in every room to keep them away.

"Hand me that pair of needles," says my grandmother. The ones in her hands have charred black smudges from where they've sparked because she knits so very fast. I do hand her the needles, but I know what she really meant was "Don't become a scientist." I find myself staring guiltily up through the ceiling and to the chemistry set in the corner of my bedroom.

I want to say "I would be a nice scientist."

I want to say "I would never unspool you, grand-mother made of yarn."

I want to say "Some scientists make things, and never destroy them."

I want to say "I can be a scientist who wears ten sweaters and hands you needles."

But I don't. Instead, I say, "Would you knit me some-thing? Maybe a purple turtleneck?" and my grand-mother smiles a stringy rainbow. She wants me to be yarny like her. Or she feels lonely being the only one. Or she loves knowing that I am warm in a cold world full of scientists. Or possibly she just wants me to have a purple turtleneck.

The yarn fire crackles. Two needles click faster and faster. Somewhere outside, a yarn hound bays.

Ruby Rorty is a writer in Chicago. Her work has appeared in *PRISM International*, *EcoTheo*, and *Red Ogre Review*, among others.

Counting

MICHELLE ROSS

One year I decided I would count the miles I ran. I succeeded for two weeks. Forty-seven miles, if you want to know. As goes with all my attempts to count, I eventually lost track. Unsure how many miles I hadn't counted, I had to estimate, which meant the counting was over because estimation is not counting. If I'm counting ants, say, and I'm not sure if the ant I see now is the same ant I saw before, my uncertainty undoes my drive to count them. I can't even begin to count macronutrients like my friend Jane, who weighs and performs a series of calculations before she puts anything into her mouth. I don't care how exact your food scale is, counting macronutrients is all an estimate. What also happens is I decide my metrics are off. What about the walk breaks I took? Should those be subtracted from my running mileage? There was a time when I kept count of the men I'd slept with. There was a time when everyone I knew did this. I remember one guy boasting that he'd slept with 101 women. He was twenty-two. He clearly didn't deliberate, as I did, as many women I knew did, about what precisely constituted sex. Counting requires conviction, commitment. It requires myopia. There's no room for nuance, for changing your mind. At book club recently, someone asked, How many times have you been in love? One woman said five times and listed off her partner and her exes. Another claimed never to have been in love. A third woman said, I don't know how many times I'm in love right this moment. Everyone else laughed, but it seemed to me the most honest answer anyone had offered. Once, traveling a back road through lush soy fields, the landscape slick and alien as birth, I came upon a lone wooden house. Without the distraction of other houses, that house seemed naked. What I mean is I don't think I'd ever really seen a house before that. Alone in my car, I felt naked, too. I'd been driving across the country to visit a man I thought I loved, a man whose face I can no longer remember. I can't remember that house's face, either, only how it undressed me, peeling away garments I hadn't even known I was wearing.

Michelle Ross is author of *There's So Much They Haven't Told You* (2017), *Shapeshifting* (2021), and *They Kept Running* (2022). Her work is anthologized in *Best Microfiction 2020, 2021,* and *2023; Best Small Fictions 2021* and *2023,* and *Flash Fiction America.* She's an editor at *100 Word Story.*

1987

CAROLYN R. RUSSELL

Bright red plastic tape crawls all over his hospital room door, and the words on it don't matter; its warning is clear. A nurse with comb-over eyebrows sees us paralyzed in front of it. *You can wait inside*, she says. *He's having some tests done.* She manages to both smile and look terrified. *We keep the door closed because, well, who knows?* "It isn't airborne" is on the tip of my tongue, but my husband squeezes my hand, and we just go in.

Carolyn R. Russell's short stories, creative nonfiction, and poetry have been featured in numerous publications. She has also authored four books, including a multi-genre flash collection called *Death and Other Survival Strategies* (Vine Leaves Press, 2023). Carolyn lives on and writes from Boston's North Shore.

The Wives of Husbands in Space

AARON SANDBERG

The wives of husbands in space gather on Sundays to talk terrestrial matters. Support-group guise, though they not-so secretly love the martyrdom—the feeling of being left on earth for some greater good. Still, left. They drag cigarettes and drink dregs of white wine before noon, orbiting each other around the kitchen. Sacrifices have been made on their ends, too. It's a quiet thrill when missions fail, though that's not quite the right word. Complications. Communication loss. They dream their husbands abort, eject, drift in the scream-silent black vacuum. Things fall apart. Centers cannot hold. The drama of breaking news sucks the oxygen from the room and they tap S.O.S. bulletins with their newly-painted nails on Formica tables. Hearing the phrase *feared dead* makes them feel alive. Distance is a rush the wives get closer to as they imagine filling voids left in their beds. *You are going to lose us before we lose you*, wives whisper to the TV, signal to each other, smile. They imagine getting what they want. Wives of husbands in space wonder how they will be when they return. Catatonic? Listless? Itching to do it again? Infected with alien disease, sleeper-cell biologies waiting to break free? Or worst of all—the same? The wives sit alone together. Have they always been like this? Strange, each thinks, blurring the boundaries of their unknown worlds, counting down to when each will wander to explore more. When each will escape the other's gravity. When each will be too far to reach for—or even to wish to come back home.

Breaker

AARON SANDBERG

The answer of course is to run fewer appliances at the same time, but she doesn't discount a supernatural cause. She runs them all to hear the hum—the low background buzz that makes her feel much less alone. But now half the house is out, the half she finds herself in, and she thinks of what she needs to do next. Her own thoughts keep bad company now that he's gone.

She thinks of all the different ways to be haunted while her sight adjusts, thinks of the believer's argument that the eye is too complex to not just be designed. But what a simple body needs is a single cell to sense the shadows—to know what to move toward or from. That's all the edge it needs.

She moves to the basement, hand tracing the wall, phone-glow guiding her steps down the stairs. She kneels in front of the panel like some sort of shrine, the switch box labeled with faded pencil from former inhabitants. And that's as ghostly as it truly gets. The reset waits. She thinks it's a form of prayer to type into the phone how to stop a circuit breaker from breaking. And maybe she's right. What else is prayer but bringing back the light or asking not to let it fade in the first place?

Some hours she believes he'll just come back. Some hours she thinks to just let go. She waits for the answers though there's no signal down here. It's a form of prayer to just be still. It's a form of prayer to be silent, asking not to be broken but whole in the dark.

Aaron Sandberg has appeared in *Rust & Moth*, *The Offing*, *Asimov's*, *Phoebe*, *Phantom Kangaroo*, *Qu*, *Alien Magazine*, and elsewhere. Nominated for The Pushcart Prize, Best of the Net, and the Dwarf Stars Award, you can see him—and his writing—on Instagram @aarondsandberg

Dead Girl Summer

SAUMYA SAWANT

Hot summer days, we perspire, existing only in those moments when your broken AC kicks to life, blows out stale cold air. Summer of our seventeenth year, we itch to discard these skins and take flight anew. I press my feet into the white of your bed sheets and wonder if this is what it feels like to rot. You lie next to me. We are two dead girls in a morgue. The skin on your thighs pulls and sticks like brown dates; I fantasize about prying them open. Later, when you hand me a red popsicle and keep the blue one for yourself, your dark eyes meeting mine, I will wonder how you knew my favorite color was purple. Outside, the sun bleaches bones white, but not here. Here, we slip our skins off, and wait.

Saumya Sawant is an Indian-American writer from New York who has been published in the *Youth Author's Anthology 2021*, the 2020 and 2022 *KSSC Anthology*, as well as the Fall '23 Issue of *Tint Journal*. In her spare time, she also runs her lifestyle blog @13oclockthoughts

Giant Silk Moth

ANGELINE SCHELLENBERG

The kind of human who can walk through a dump and see wings, Michelle believes people make too much of distinctions: hair vs. headscarf, bike vs. cane, breast vs. scar the shape of the crescent moon. Butterfly or moth—both so beautiful. Even caterpillars, she thinks, wrapping her quilt tighter.

Angeline Schellenberg is the author of *Tell Them It Was Mozart* (2016), *Fields of Light and Stone* (2020), and *Mondegreen Riffs* (2024). She serves as a contemplative spiritual director, second shooter for Anthony Mark Photography, and host of the Speaking Crow poetry open mic in Winnipeg, Canada.

Marie-Antoinette's Nose

DONNA SHANLEY

The Parfumeur's proboscis preceded him like a ship's prow, nostrils flared to invite the perfumes of the world. She'd giggle sometimes, imagining them as sails, capturing the scented wind. He'd inhale slowly, eyes closed, his expression rapturous or offended, then utter a word: "jonquil," "sandalwood," "rhubarb," "rat." The right word, always. *Her* nose—not too short for queenliness, a trifle long for elegance, perhaps (sneering voices muttered that one needed a certain length of nose in order to look down it)—would dip briefly in deference to his brilliance. It deferred to nothing else.

Powdered and pampered, it reveled in the cloud-like sweetness of macarons, the rich musk of velvet; wrinkled delightedly at the tickle of champagne. It hovered, enchanted, over the milky scent of a baby's skin; luxuriated in amber and almond, wafting warm from the bath. If the indiscreet pomade on a Duke's coiffure made it sneeze, it sought the comfort of lace-edged linen, sprinkled with lavender.

On this day, though, on *this* day, it recoiled, a trapped

animal, from the onion-reek of taunting mouths. And from something else—salty, rusty, terrible—splattered on the unforgiving oak. Even the roses, breathed in secret from the smuggled flask, could never have disguised a perfume like this: a perfume that barely paused at the nose before it flew to set the heart thudding, the brain reeling.

The Parfumeur, weeping alone in the cell, knew the word for it: *heady*.

Donna Shanley studied literature at Simon Fraser University, and wild orangutans in Borneo. She lives in Vancouver, Canada, where she can almost always see mountains. Her fiction appears in *Vestal Review*, *Ellipsis Zine*, *Flash Frontier*, *Milk Candy Review*, *The Ekphrastic Review*, *MacQueen's Quinterly*, *The Citron Review*, and *NUNUM*.

October Again

BETH SHERMAN

Bark peels off the maples. Leaves wither and die, everyone says how beautiful. Sedum turning a muddy green, like rotten asparagus. Nights, the man at the end of the court wanders by, his gun tucked into his waistband. Moonlight nests in his hair, bounces off his angry face. Since you left, spiders have colonized the pantry, racing each other for fun. The bedroom window leaks, a muffled plunk-plunk-plunk. When I try to imagine where you are, it always involves flight: Wings loosening. The moment when the mallard shows its silvery throat, gliding under clouds before the first shot is fired.

Beth Sherman has an MFA in creative writing from Queens College, where she teaches in the English department. Her stories have appeared in *Portland Review*, *Blue Mountain Review*, *100 Word Story*, *Fictive Dream*, *Flash Boulevard*, and elsewhere. She is a Pushcart Prize, Best Small Fictions, and a multiple Best of the Net nominee.

Parallel

KELLI SHORT BORGES

I wonder what would have happened if we hadn't gone that day. If, instead of grabbing car keys we had grabbed each other, your breath hot against my cheek as you whispered, "Let's stay home instead." After, we would nestle, honey-limbed, on our worn love seat, Billie Eilish breathy like a promise on the old forty-five. We'd toast your birthday with Two Buck Chuck in yard sale glasses, never missing the Michelin star crystal. You would push your feet into my palms, groaning in pleasure as I warmed them. The car still whole, in the garage. Your blood-red toes, untagged.

Hive

KELLI SHORT BORGES

Mandy says she's queen of seventh grade and we're her workers and she "ha ha ha's," but her eyes flash venom and it's annoying because Mandy's the new girl and already thinks she's royalty but she's so pretty that we *whirr* around her, happy because it's Friday night and her parents are out of town not hovering like ours and we're getting our buzz on, stolen Hennessy from the liquor cabinet sweet on our tongues, and we slick on lavender-scented gloss, practice kissing, braces tangling, tongues proboscis-swirling pretending it's Jesse, the hottest guy at school, and Mandy says "back off, he's mine," because she's queen and we dart away— stingers out, antennae quivering—then remember from Mr. Gary's science class when new queens stress the workers they surround her inside a burning mass and when she dies her body's thrown from the hive, so we swarm Mandy, scorching, waiting for her to ignite.

Kelli Short Borges writes fiction from her home in Phoenix, Arizona. Her work has been nominated for multiple awards and published in journals such as *The Dribble Drabble Review*, *The Citron Review*, *Cleaver*, *The Penn Review*, *Your Impossible Voice*, and elsewhere. She is currently working on her first novel.

There Are Four Words For 'You' In the Malay Language

SUMITRA SINGAM

I called you 'anda' when we first met. The pink shell of your mouth made a pearl of an assalamualaikum for me. Our husbands were in the front room, and we went to the kitchen, sitting cross-legged with our feet tucked away for respect. I brought us a plate of piping hot jemput-jemput and you ate the sugary fritters, blowing through your mouth, using your hand like a fan. Your fingers seemed plump, juicy, like the succulents in my garden. I wondered if they would feel as soft and pliant to touch.

When we met at that satay place in Kajang, the air full of the smoky, earthy smell of roasting meat, I called you 'awak.' I said, awak tak bosan? You said, no, you weren't bored when your husband was away so much for work, and I wondered if I was a particularly ungrateful kind of wife. You said, can I try? pointing at my glass of pink bandung gently sweating in the humidity. You pursed your lips perfectly around the straw, taking greedy gulps. After you left, I fitted my mouth as closely as I could to the ring of bright red lipstick on the straw.

When I invited you to Port Dickson, I called you 'kamu.' We bought rambutan from a roadside stall, and I made a joke about how the hairy fruit looked just like testicles. You frowned and swatted my arm, but your dimples peeked out anyway. We took a mat down to the beach, our bare feet crunching into the sand. I shelled the rambutans, handing them to you one by one. You popped the oval fruit, translucent like lychees into your mouth, making throaty sounds of pleasure. You pulled out clean seeds which you gathered in a pile on the sand.

I called you 'engkau' when you invited me to your place for lunch. We ate assam fish and rice, your right hand making a perfect bud when you gathered a mouthful together. Your food tasted like everything – spicy, sweet, tart, buttery. You called me 'engkau' then too. We reached for the dish at the same time, our hands brushing together, warm and soft. You didn't snatch your hand away. You didn't say the word 'haram.' What you did say was, it's beautiful, the Malay phrase for pronoun, 'kata ganti diri.' A word to replace yourself.

Sumitra Singam is a Malaysian-Indian-Australian coconut who writes in Naarm/Melbourne. She travelled through many spaces, both beautiful and traumatic, to get there and writes to make sense of her experiences. She'll be the one in the kitchen making chai (where's your cardamom?). She works in mental health.

Everything is Flat

L. SOVIERO

Flat building. Flat windows. Flat sky. Flat sun.

Alex kicks a can. It ricochets off the building wall. Chips away the white paint, creating a fresh wound of the red brick below. Above the rift, his eyes drift to an open window on the ground floor. A window that leads into the apartment of an old man with a ski slope back. With a face permanently scowled. Once I asked mom why he looked that way, and she said that's how some people ended up when they missed others and were not themselves missed.

Alex lifts himself on the sill to peek inside the old man's home. When he's sure the coast is clear, he picks up a slice of newspaper, balls it and throws it inside. Next, an empty can, which yelps tinnily as it hits the kitchen tiles. The rest of us nervous titter and for Alex that's enough of a pat on the back as he darts down the alley and returns with a broken-necked beer bottle and lobs that in too. A few of us laugh again as it shatters, but more of us shuffle our Keds and our Reeboks and suggest playing manhunt or hide-and-seek instead. But Alex is already returning from the basement by then, lugging a bloated garbage bag, which he splits open like the belly of some beast. The insides spilling out putrid: mushy tomatoes, diseased banana peels, leaky milk cartons, cracked eggshells still oozing their yolks and our heads shake no no no as he bundles it up and forces it through the window. After, keeling with laughter so intense spit gathers in the corners of his mouth as he hugs his gut.

And then the old man is in the alley too, his slope making him appear the same size as us. The worn brown suit and old-fashioned hat. That brown cane, like a giant finger pointing at us as he shouts. Alex dancing around him, dodging that waggling finger. Some of us run away as Alex taunts him. Others watch from a distance with our hearts thumping off beat. Others look down at our crisp, new sneakers again as the old man palms his chest. And we watch the ski slope back slope nearer to the glass-spattered ground of the alley. And hear the siren that we will later swear was wailing *you you you you* to anyone in its path. Just like the cane. That finger pointing.

L. Soviero is a writer from Queens, living in Melbourne. Her work has been nominated for Best of the Net and Best Small Fictions. Additionally, she has been longlisted at *Wigleaf* and her story "Lucy Ignores Death" was spotlighted in *Best Small Fictions 2021*.

Flemish Tavern

PHILLIP STERLING

He tells me that if you were a sniper in Belgium during the war, you wanted to be in the Ardennes when the rations ran out—there were still rabbits and squirrels in the mountains—and not in the low country, where the only heights were undamaged windmills, and you fished eels out of the canals. It was the big difference, he says, like—how do you say?—heaven and hell. The waiter places the bowl in front of me, its fishy green stew. Now, he says, eel's a delicacy, if properly prepared. Isn't that the way of every war?

Phillip Sterling's books include *In Which Brief Stories Are Told* (short fiction, Wayne State U Press), *Amateur Husbandry* (micro-fiction, Mayapple), and five collections of poetry, most recently *Local Congregation: Poems Uncollected 1985-2015* (Main Street Rag, October 2023).

I AM NOT AFRAID OF TRANSSEXUALS

JOHN ELIZABETH STINTZI

As a new emergency law goes into effect, a step toward making my existence illegal, I walk into a sporting goods store in Liberty, Missouri and buy a semi-automatic target pistol.

The woman behind the counter doesn't mind my lavender nails. The spoon rings on my fingers. She puts pistols in my hands. She upsells me. I buy three cartons of rounds. I'm in and out in fifteen minutes.

South on Highway 71, five miles over the speed limit, I cannot tell which part of me is paranoia and which is pattern recognition. The gun sits in my lap, in my hand, pointing at the empty passenger seat. The safety is on, but yes: she's loaded. She smells amazing.

I'll name the gun Liberty and she'll sleep beside me in bed. I'll walk her with my dog, every day, through a neighborhood that has always felt safe. I'll bring her to the gym where I'll learn Muay Thai from a local flyweight champion. She'll wait for me in the locker room where I'll pretend to be a man.

I'll reach for Liberty nervously, at first, then habitually, in the way one learns to reach for a cellphone. I'll begin to long for the country, where I can plink cans any time of day. I'll long to print out little photos of fascists to put on the face of every can I plink. I'll clean Liberty every week, even the rare weeks I do not fire her.

I'll get on a first name basis with a man at a shooting range in Raytown. I'll put on lipstick. People will give me looks, but I'll become a markswoman. I'll cap every angel on the head of a pin.

As I drive home, the world widens. Sharpens. There's a future for me, and people like me, somewhere out here. It smells of gunmetal.

John Elizabeth Stintzi (they/she) is the award-winning author of the novels *My Volcano* and *Vanishing Monuments*, the poetry collection *Junebat*, and the new short story collection *Bad Houses*. They are currently illustrating their first graphic novel: *Automaton Deactivation Bureau*.

Pancakes

KRISTIN TENOR

She doesn't know why her mother walked barefoot to the neighbor's pond that day or why she set the rowboat adrift or why she lay in the bottom of it dressed in her blue terrycloth bathrobe with an anchor tied around her slim, white ankle like a string tethered to a runaway kite. She wonders how long she waited for the sun to rise or if she instead stared intently at a hawk floating in wide, lazy circles above her. She also wonders why her father didn't run after her, why he stayed behind to make pancakes while she and Lucie wailed along with Patsy Cline singing "Crazy" over the turquoise AM radio plugged into the wall beside the percolating coffee pot and two empty mugs sitting side by side with their handles pointed away from one another. She doesn't know why they didn't ask where their mother had gone so early on a Sunday morning or why they hadn't been told to change into their dresses and Mary Janes so they wouldn't be late for the 8:15 service at Old St. Joe's. She doesn't know why they didn't miss her. Maybe they were too caught up watching their father flip pancakes into the air, higher and higher, like a carnival performer. They ran around the kitchen, holding their plates, trying to keep the perfect cakes from hitting the tacky linoleum floor, where their father's mangy coonhound, Melchizedek, would surely ravage them whole. She and Lucie may only have been six and seven, but they knew how gravity worked.

Kristin Tenor finds inspiration in life's quiet details and believes in their power to illuminate the extraordinary. Her fiction has appeared in *Wigleaf, X-R-A-Y, Bending Genres, Emerge Literary Journal*, and elsewhere. Her work has also been nominated for Best of the Net, Best Small Fictions, and the Pushcart Prize as well as longlisted in the *Wigleaf* Top 50. Read more at www.kristintenor.com.

Dictatorship of the Proletariat

FÉLIX TERRONES

*translated from the Spanish
by Andrea Reece*

He noticed it the first damn time he saw me. That imperceptible tremor brought on by the sight of a beggar, which, once I saw the glint in his eyes, transformed into a secret, unsettling and lethal sense of power. Yet I was able to act as if nothing were wrong, casually adjusting my jacket, searching with exaggerated care for a coin in my pocket, and letting it drop obligingly into his pot (recalling this, my actions seem ludicrously over the top, but at the time they calmed me). Needless to say, I bumped into him the following day, and again the one after. Eventually, I resigned myself to giving him a coin every morning, until one day he decided he wanted a banknote instead, or, preferably, my wallet. He subsequently claimed my jacket, and then my shirt. When he demanded my briefcase containing the firm's documents, checks and promissory notes, I gritted my teeth—I still remember the rage and determination in his eyes. I have nothing left to give but my house keys, which is why I don't want to see him this morning. Yet when I spot him on the street, standing tall and smartly dressed, he's impossible to resist. I grovel along the ground so he deigns to notice the keys he has dropped. I think he glances at me, but maybe he doesn't. As I watch him vanish round the corner with his briefcase and his keys, I pick up the coin he tossed me and scuttle away to hide among the rats and the cockroaches. That is where I belong.

Félix Terrones (Lima, Peru) is a scholar, teacher, translator and writer of novels, short stories and microfiction, including *El viento en tu cara* (2014, Nazarí) from which the translated piece included here is taken. He holds a PhD from the Université de Bordeaux (France) on brothels in the Latin-American novel.

Andrea Reece (Brighton, UK) is a French and Spanish to English translator of fiction, non-fiction and children's books including a *Sunday Times* bestseller and a winner of a Pen Translates award. She holds an MA in Literary Translation from Exeter University (UK) and lives in England and the French Pyrenees.

Last Seen

Eric Scot Tryon

I put the first *Missing* flier up early Saturday morning. Pinned to a telephone pole, and overlapped between a Garage Sale sign and a Lost Cat poster, was my sister's smiling face. A school photo with a fake mountain background. The garage sale promised fine oak furniture. The lost cat—Mr. Blueberry—had a striped tail and needed medication. My sister was declared to be "5'1, 112 lbs." All these years and I had never known her weight. Not that it's a thing brothers know. Just felt odd to see it for the first time. 112. Seemed like a big number, in bold ink, sitting on its own, but she was a small girl.

By lunch I had made my way to the Safeway over on Grant and Steiner. There was a corkboard by the CoinStar. This time I squeezed her between a For Sale flier for a pickup truck and an advertisement for piano lessons with the little tabs at the bottom to rip off if interested. The truck had 145,000 miles on it. The piano lessons were $80 an hour, but the lady had gone to Julliard. My sister's birthday was "09/13/06." Written like that made it look more like an account number than a celebration with balloons, streamers, and ice cream cake, always mint chocolate chip.

The sun was setting by the time I hung the last flier on the Community Board at the entrance of McSweeney Park. There wasn't a single inch of open space, so I tacked the flier over an announcement for T-Ball sign ups. Ages 5-9, no experience necessary. But now that space read: "Last Seen: Wednesday at 2:50 leaving St. Vincent's High School." As I pushed the pins in, I could feel the board swollen with paper. The original cork a distant memory.

As I turned to leave I noticed another flier for Mr. Blueberry peeking out from between two ripped yellow soccer posters. This one looked much older. How long had Mr. Blueberry been gone? Or maybe he was found and his owners were so happy they forgot to take down the signs. Or maybe they never found him and instead spent their lives stapling new fliers over old fliers over older fliers.

And when was Mr. Blueberry last seen? The flier didn't say. And who was it that saw him? At least in his case, it wasn't me.

At A Roadside Attraction On The Brink Of Divorce

Eric Scot Tryon

We watch the circus flea do backflips. We watch the circus flea juggle fire and swallow tiny swords. With buttery hands buried in popcorn, we squint into the bright lights of the shoebox stage and try to find meaning in the smallest of things. In toothpick stilts and button unicycles. Fleas are blind, you whisper to me as the circus flea lifts a golf ball over its head with ease. But they can sense the slightest vibrations, you whisper as the circus flea is shot from a tiny cannon. The circus flea is strong and brave and all the things we are not.

But come the finale, the circus flea trembles atop the paperclip ladder. A foot above the stage, it shakes as it takes a blind step onto the thin gray hair stretched taut from end to end. The tightrope is an eternity. You mumble a prayer under your popcorn breath and kiss the cross around your neck. You care so damn much for the circus flea. And as it moves its six legs one in front of the other, teetering on the edge of a freefall, I close my eyes, hold my breath, and stop my heart. Hoping that maybe, if I'm still enough, I will feel your vibration and know what it means.

Eric Scot Tryon is a writer and editor from San Francisco. His work has been selected for the *Wigleaf* Top 50 and the *Best Small Fictions* anthology. Eric is represented by Carleen Geisler at ArtHouse Literary Agency. He is also the Founding Editor of *Flash Frog*.

Flotsam

Rebecca Turkewitz

In April, the sea began to leave us strange things. An ivory comb. A tortoiseshell headband. A potato masher. A key. When the tide receded each day, the objects would be strewn across the beaches or caught in the marsh grass. Our kids, splashing in tide pools, found cat-eye glasses, a waterlogged copy of *Little Women,* a plastic ring looped around the shell of a periwinkle. Bill Fryer pulled up a lobster trap full of high-heeled shoes. We figured there'd been a shipwreck somewhere far from our little island town.

We collected the objects and arranged them on the library lawn. Then, Laura Goldstein spotted her grandmother's pearl necklace with its broken clasp. We opened the copy of *Little Women* and read, "Property of Molly Shields," who was a deckhand on the ferry.

We called a meeting. We claimed the objects that were ours and returned them to bedside drawers or kitchen cabinets or cardboard boxes in basements and garages.

Soon, the beaches were so thick with detritus we couldn't take our morning walks.

We debated. We gossiped. We searched for patterns. We tried to treasure our belongings. Then, we tried to give up worldly things. We never noticed that the objects were missing until the sea gave them back. We drank tea or whiskey to calm our nerves. We had trouble sleeping. When we slept, we dreamed of waves.

We started combing the beaches. We took whatever we wanted. Some of us made orderly piles to contain the mess. Some made altars or structures like cairns. A few flung everything they found right back into the ocean. Some refused to touch the items at all. We worried what would happen come tourist season.

Then, one Tuesday in early June, the beaches were clear.

It hadn't stormed the night before. The morning wasn't especially foggy, or cloudless, or warm. Sometimes the sea takes on an unusual color in the morning or stills so much that the surface is like glass. But that day there was nothing remarkable, except that the tideline was clear. We bent closer, kicking aside thick mats of gray-green seaweed, but there were no yo-yos or coasters or sodden scarves.

We didn't know how to feel. We were relieved, of course, but there was something left behind, a suspicion we couldn't identify or shake. We thought we would sleep better, but for years we did not.

Rebecca Turkewitz is a writer and high school teacher living in Maine. She is the author of the story collection *Here in the Night* (Black Lawrence Press). Her fiction and humor have appeared in *Electric Literature*, *SmokeLong Quarterly*, *Alaska Quarterly Review*, *Pithead Chapel*, *The New Yorker's Daily Shouts*, and elsewhere.

Stargazey Pie

RICK WHITE

I bake the pie every year on your birthday, yes it seems a strange thing to do; but we were always strange, and strangeness is a thing worth carrying. I cut the tails off the pilchards and stand them in the dish, eggs and potatoes next. The fish are firm and fresh, loaded off the dock this morning. The eyes, shiny and bright. I drape the pastry over them, cut holes for the heads. Bake.

Your bedroom door was locked from the outside, but you learned to pick the window-latch from within. I'd wait below to catch you when you dropped. We'd walk to the harbour, sometimes out to the estuary where on cold, clear nights all the constellations were visible. You told me Pegasus was your favourite: the great, winged horse galloping across the night sky, foaled from the neck of Medusa as she lay dying, slain by Perseus. I still don't know how you knew that.

At Christmas we'd go to see the harbour lights, disappear into the crowd with a stolen bottle of vodka. All the old fishermen with their wrinkled, leathery faces and rough, barnacled knuckles like your dad, too drunk to notice us. We'd walk to the edge of the town and share our secrets with the gulls — the chattering, indifferent throng. Said one day we'd disappear, set sail and never look back.

I still search for Pegasus in the night sky, and I ask myself the same question over and over: how did you sneak back into your room?

They found you in the harbour, wrapped in a trawler's net. Said you might've drifted for days, only to end up right back where you started. I saw them pull you from the spray, saw you green and draped in seaweed. Heard the gulls sing a shanty as they covered you up.

I said I hadn't seen you, but I did look. Now the fish look up to the heavens, and maybe you'll see their eyes twinkle down below. Sometimes I go missing too. I take a bottle with me and dream of sinking into the heedless memory of the sea. When I get home, I half expect you to've picked my lock, and be there waiting for me in my kitchen. But there is only ever the smell of fish gone bad, and eyes that no longer shine.

Rick White lives and writes in Manchester, UK. His debut short fiction collection *Talking to Ghosts at Parties* is available now.

Not the End of the World

NAN WIGINGTON

Nobody believed Jo when she told us about the butterflies, how they broke from the flare's black hood, their lacy wings fluttering past the empty train cars, over the fence, and onto our dirt pan lawns. One landed on her right arm and sizzled like a lit cigarette. Couldn't we see the scar? Smell the sulphur?

Even her mother shook her head. And her father, who was buttoning his coat, yawned, ruffled his girl's hair, and walked down the streets to the refinery.

Jo tried to keep the spiders a secret but couldn't help herself. She told us how they emerged from a tear in a tank, a black spill of furry legs, jaws, and abdomens crowding into the air, spreading along the creek, floating on the water, out through the tunnel, and under the highway.

Jo said the end was coming. Seven years old, and she's all Armageddon. As if living in the shadow of the refinery isn't going to test our souls. Like we don't know, the company is demon and god, a giver of paychecks and debt, life and death.

We did see the rats, a vaporous trail from a distillation tower, scurrying in a line down, up, down across the pipes, and finally into the weeds.

"It's coming," Jo said.

But we all went to bed.

In the morning, the explosion rocked our front doors open and filled the sky with orange heat and hissing flames. Metal twisted, turned white, and rose like bones from a grave. Plastic melted and dripped red onto the roads. Towers tumbled. Valves visited rooftops and burned holes through slate shingles.

The refinery told the newspapers it was a minor setback. Repairs would only take a day, a month, a week. No one was to blame. Unless it was one of the night's workers, someone who got sleepy and made a mistake. Probably Jo's father. Hadn't we all foreseen it? There he was — so many overtime hours — reaching for the wrong switch, the ignition launching his body through the combusting sky, punching a hole in heaven.

Nan Wigington is honored to be part of this collection and grateful to Geoffrey Miller, as well as NUNUM, for finding a place for her work. She lives in the Rocky Mountain West near a cemetery and an oil refinery.

We walked out of the forest

FRANCINE WITTE

And Tooley, who doesn't like the forest, says loud and clear into the frostbell air, can't we go to a movie for a change?

I've been trying all kinds of whatever with Tooley. Dress-me-up sex and now hiking, that I had to buy a pair of boots for.

I say, Tooley, just look at that house over there in the clearing. Tooley tells me I sound like a fairy tale. The clearing, Tooley says with his Tooley-sneer, who talks like that in real life?

Excuse me, mister, I say trying to be light and all, but I talk like that. And it's a beautiful clearing, a beautiful house. Look at that sloping roof, all white and Christmas. I bet a wonderful family lives there.

We are a wonderful family, Tooley says, and I figure he's being sarcastic, so I tell him right there that he is the one sounding like a fairy tale. He rears back at that, like a unicorn heaving up on its hind legs. I give you everything, Tooley says. And by everything, I say, I am sure you mean heartache. I remind him right there about Loretta. Which is a thing he would rather I forget.

The trees all around us are scabby and bare, the grass nearly dead and glistened with snowfrost. Without the forest to hush up our thoughts, Tooley and I can hear everything we are thinking at each other.

I'm going to knock on that door, I tell Tooley. I bet there's a warm fire there, and cocoa.

Well, I'm going home. Tooley says and walks away from me like he's done so many times. I watch him fade back into the forest. I watch and watch until he is a twig himself.

I walk across the open field. Sprinkle of ice cracking under my boots. I am hoping that if there isn't a family inside of that house, then maybe a kindly old woman, someone who will make me feel wanted and make me feel loved, the way I must have felt the first time I looked into Tooley's eyes.

At worst, it will be a poisoned apple that I will at least know enough not to bite.

Francine Witte is the author of eleven books of poetry and flash fiction. Her flash fiction collection *RADIO WATER* was published by Roadside Press in January 2024. She is flash fiction editor of *FLASH BOULEVARD* and *South Florida Poetry Journal*. Visit her website at francinewitte.com

Buying Snowball Pumpkins in Athens, Tennessee

WILLIAM KELLEY WOOLFITT

My sons wrong-turn in the corn maze, then shriek at light-up skeletons, plastic bones, neon green spider webs. I'm ignoring the gnat-like hum of worry-nerves in my chest. There's tire mountain, there's sliding hill the boys zoom down, I'm not testing the weather, not wondering about the sun, the heat, is it mild today, yolk-yellow, not too bright, not too warm. I'm trying to look carefully, see only tractor ride, zip line, my sons at the hay jump, the pig race. Sara and Maybelle sing, when the world's on fire, tide me over in the rock of ages. Not long ago, in the Mountain State, a hundred-year-flood: the Elk River guzzled all the rain, swallowed bridges and roads, spread trash and mud everywhere, ruined the houses of families who then had to live in campers and tents on Walgrove Road, at Blue Creek. Not long ago, the coal-washing foam that Freedom Industries spilled into the Elk, whiff of licorice in the tap water, nausea and rashes, diamond darters the spill may have wiped out. Not long ago, derecho, hard winds, no electricity on the hottest day of summer, senator from my hometown siding with fossil fuels again. I'm buying sprinkle donuts for my sons to eat on the way home, I'm not feeling buzz in my chest, lump in my stomach. Maggie Anderson says, it's hard for a river to carve a valley, pulling toward the sea on its hands and knees. My sons ask me to name what they see out the windows: paper mill, vinyl goblins, skulls that glow. There's Mouse Creek, crystalline stone, patch of clear sky, what might be earthly, little, still free.

William Woolfitt is the author of four poetry collections, two story collections, and an essay collection. *Ring of Earth* (stories) was published by Madville Publishing in 2023; *The Night the Rain Had Nowhere to Go* (poems) was published by Belle Point Press in 2024.

The No Longer Girls
(A Song Unsung)

JEN WYRAUCH EDSON

The No Longer Girls possessed older boyfriends and carried so many keys. They shouldered off-white, macramé satchels, starving and deep enough for most departures. Fake ids, Aqua Net, one apple, The Pill, and waterproof makeup. The No Longer Girls carried tampons, not pads, Obsession over Love's Baby Soft. They laughed at our curfews but wished for just one. They coded calendars and kept unfinished poems; they watched watches. They carried checkbooks, claimed awareness of balances and costs.

The No Longer Girls carried key chains round as bracelet bangles; the keys, those badges, those hard-won dishonors, clung like charms, sang a jangled song like freedom: the right key, the right lock. The keys glittered from same ring, copper challenging silver, silver scratching gold; they winked in stolen sunlight, never fell from display, or our envy, at the farthest edge of The No Longer Girls desks.

The No Longer Girls, often marked absent when present, held space differently. Their attention trained on some distant shore: a silence called safety.

The No Longer Girls said balancing ledges was easy; you could walk the line on either side of a white picket fence, just know what side you're on. They did not speak of exits or losing agency, clinics or contingencies. How locks can all change in one kind of blue night. After the inked signatures, after statements copied on straight lines, still as babies uncarried. College acceptances sealed. Events escaped for the privilege of waiting on some star-struck street corner, along Pacific Coast Highway above Strands Beach.

The No Longer Girls knew the weight silence carried. The voiced I miss you, dangerous as a dropped birth control pill, a diaphragm misplaced, a red light run. The L-word, always much too heavy. A locked door, a broken key. A song unsung.

Jen Wyrauch Edson holds an MFA in Fiction from Antioch University, Los Angeles, and was awarded residencies at Dorland Mountain Arts Colony. She teaches remotely and lives in Chico, California, and Palm Desert with two very good dogs and her beloved husband, Paul. She is currently writing a memoir.

When He Heard about the Y2K Bug

ADDISON ZELLER

Dad added forty or fifty canned hams to the family. He brought in another two each grocery run, stacked them along the wall by the sump pump. I just thought of something, we'll need a kerosene lamp—he said that kind of thing to Mom, as they lay in bed. That lamp, canned food for two years, propane tanks, a portable grill: all safely hidden in the only room with no access to natural light. He'd flick off the switch and creep around in there like an ancient Celt inspecting his souterrain. This is how it'll be, he said. The dog circled his feet, excited by the dark. I'm doing this for you, Dad told it, so we won't have to eat you. His face glowed orange over the glass-lamp chimney. He was proud and happy—the proudest and happiest I ever saw him. He kept a metal box in a wall crack by the furnace. Sometimes I peered in and saw the key sticking out of the lock. He would take it out and show me the handgun. It was an obsession with him: I even got to hold it so long as he kept his fingers on the butt. People will notice who has food and who doesn't, he said. That's the thing.

He had a plan for us. We'd sleep in the finished part of the basement, and he'd get up to do his rounds at midnight, then closer to dawn I'd do mine. That's how it'd be. We'd listen at the windows, make sure the doors were locked tight. Just us and the dog and the lamp and the gun. Then we'd go down again and fall back to sleep while the others slept on.

The hams dreamed in their silver caskets like dead bandits out for display in a Western town.

Addison Zeller's fiction appears in *3:AM*, *Epiphany*, *Pithead Chapel*, *trampset*, *minor literature[s]*, *LIGEIA*, *hex*, *ergot.*, and elsewhere. He lives in Wooster, Ohio, and edits fiction for *The Dodge*.

There is No Gold Here

ELENA ZHANG

When I was young, my father loved to tell me the story of the man who buried gold in his backyard. Worried about thieves, he drove a sign in the ground next to the freshly turned earth, one that read, "There is no gold here." The next day, the gold was gone. My father loved to laugh at the man's foolishness. I loved to hear my father laugh. Neither of us knew that years later, when my father buried my mother in the backyard, he would become the signpost planted in the soil, a scarecrow of blank eyes and jagged teeth warning me away, there is no gold here, there is no gold here. He stretched out his arms as if he was going to hug me, but I was no fool. I kicked him until he fell over, and began to dig for treasure with my hands, clawing into the soft, damp chocolate cookie crumbs, finding no gummy worms, no mother either. I kept digging. Soon, crows began to peck at my father's straw face. They swallowed jelly eyes and spat out pearl teeth. *There is no gold here* became *old ear, old ear, oh dear, oh dear.* I dug until my fingers turned raw pink like wounds, like a heart. I dug until I became the gaping hole's wriggling tongue, until my father's laughter sounded like caws. *Hao hao hao.* Good good good.

Elena Zhang is a Chinese American writer and mother living in Chicago. Her work can be found in *HAD, JAKE, Exposition Review, Your Impossible Voice,* and *Gone Lawn,* among other publications.

ESSAYS & INSIGHTS

When a Picture is Worth 400 words

Eric Scot Tryon

In reflecting on the origin and writing of both stories lucky enough to be included in this wonderful anthology, I realized the process was actually quite similar. A process I might not have been aware of at the time, but isn't discovery the beauty of reflection?

Both stories came from the flash of a brief, fleeting image that caught my attention. "At a Roadside Attraction on the Brink of Divorce" came about when I was mindlessly scrolling social media and happened upon a photograph of a tiny circus. A big fan of small, bizarre subcultures, I knew I had to write a story that takes place at a flea circus. "Last Seen" began when I was at a coffee shop and noticed a community bulletin board swollen with flyers: items for sale, lessons offered, pets missing, and I knew I had to write a story that takes place on public bulletin boards.

But then the real work starts. Who was at this flea circus? And why? What would they get from it? And who was tacking new fliers on the town's corkboards. And why? What were they looking for, wanting, missing?

And then one draft becomes four, and characters start to emerge. I begin to see them and get to know their inner workings, and they eventually become real people, their tiny stories taking shape.

Lastly, I focus on language and rhythm and pacing. For me, these are the lifeblood of flash, and so for months, I agonize over every word and read the piece aloud over and over until I've reached the point of diminishing return.

So by the end, what I'm left with is a story about a married couple that have grown so distant from one another they no longer can read each other's tone, expression, body language. And a story about a young boy whose sister has gone missing as he frantically tries to navigate this tragedy the only way he knows how. But I think if I had started the other way around—set out from the beginning to write a story about a couple on the brink of divorce or a story about a missing girl and her brother—I don't think I could have arrived at nearly the same place or with the same energy.

So am I doing things backwards? Forwards? Who's to say?

Story is Always There

KELLI SHORT BORGES

Picture a film on the big screen, maybe one of those old-fashioned theatres with red velvet curtains. As you crunch your popcorn, a young woman looms on the screen, her limp hair an unfortunate brown. Glasses slide down the hump of her nose. Her outfit screams "grandma chic," but it's not yet 2024 and she's anything but chic. The hot guy in school, *standing right there*, is asking her to dance. She looks behind her, sure Tiffany the cheerleader's there, but no, it's *her* he's asking. *She blinks...*

That woman? She's me. To be asked to write an essay contributing to this anthology, a brilliant compilation of stories by writers I respect and admire, feels like the literary equivalent of that scene. I'm incredibly honored.

For me, stories surface in two ways, spontaneously (rare and wonderful, those that seem to tell themselves), or through workshops. Prompts are just igniters that spark the kindling of our subconscious. Story is always there, waiting.

I'm forever fascinated with how the tiniest choices we make can change the future completely, which was the seed for "Parallel." It started with a critique group challenge—to weave "I wonder what would have happened if…" into a story. Nothing immediately surfaced, so I tucked it away. I pulled it out again months later as I was taking a workshop, and voila! Of course, honing the piece wasn't quite that easy. Multiple drafts and adding unexpected language and sensory details followed. I'd like to note, here, that Nicole Brogdon's brilliant story, "Pastels," included in this anthology, was also born from that same critique group prompt. Big fan of prompts, here, and of smart writerly friends.

Crafting "Hive," also written in a workshop, was really fun. I vividly remember being a teenager—the hormones, the insecurities, the yearning. The one-sentence breathless paragraph structure came naturally, urgency dictated the form. Put some unsupervised teen girls together, add alcohol, jealousy, and competition, and you have the recipe for a swarm. The ending was a bit harder to nail. I slowed down and researched bees. I found that the worker bees literally throw a new queen out when they don't accept her, and she dies. *Perfect.*

The final step for me is always sending my best rough draft to critique partners whose opinions I trust. It's my favorite thing about writing—sharing stories and learning with each other!

On Craft

KEN POYNER

Knowledge can be transformative, or not. In both of these pieces, there is a decision point propelling characters into where they fit in the given circumstance. In "Beautification," the resistance of the boy indicates to the bettor that the boy will do well and is worth the bet. In "Proof," the student who wishes to be a clownherd understands he has to study clowns to herd them – but if he studies too closely, he is in danger of becoming a clown: and a herd of clowns is not best led by one of their own. One might think that obedience in the boy would make him a better fighter, but the bettor knows it is the boy's unwillingness to submit that will make the bettor money; and the prospective clownherd understands that he must stand out from those he wishes to herd to be successful.

Philosophical method has always posited absurd circumstances to sharpen the edges of moral decision. I hope to use the absurd to remove practical complaints and instead focus on the choices being made by the obtuse characters in my unreal situations. Betting on boys in a fight, or trying to herd clowns, creates a field where other principles can be isolated and aired.

Hopefully, there is space for the reader to independently consider the morality of fighting boys or herding clowns, but these are not questions for the characters in the stories.

For inspiration, I look at how humanity is configured. Much of our social existence is committed to recognizing hierarchies. Many of our actions are undertaken to establish place. Such has always been the case, but modern complexities compound perspective and conflict. We are insecure individuals always trying to prove that we have position within the herd, or at the head of the herd. The bettor understands how the boy will distinguish himself. The clownherd knows he cannot identify too closely with his charges. Separation, not solidarity, is success. We all need to show we have the secret.

On Writing

L MARI HARRIS

Most of my writing is done in my head before I ever start typing. An image, a conflict, or a phrase will come to me, and I'll free associate—what I call imagination meandering—letting thoughts and memories rise to the surface—some leading to locked doors, some leading to open windows.

Each of my micros had their beginnings in different ways. "Our Mothers" came from the opening line "slow dance to sad songs," and that led me, in that inevitable Proustian way, to remember so many of my friends' mothers, who, to a young girl, were all so glamorous, dressing up on a Saturday night in their polyester pantsuits and high heels, drugstore perfume wafting throughout the house, as they clicked out their doors and headed to the local bar, leaving us girls (kids, really) to fend for ourselves (oh, the freedom!), and yet I also observed many days when my friends' houses had no electricity or running water until enough money could be found (somehow, it always was found) to turn the utilities back on, until it all circled around again and they were back to square one. Today, we would probably call this neglect, how eight-year-olds were left alone at night, the scarcity of food, the times when there was no heat in the house. And yet I wanted to pay homage to these women, who were survivors, who still dreamed when dreaming didn't pay the bills.

For "Something Inside Us Rises Up" I was driving behind a chicken truck one day, and a chicken fell out of one of the open-air cages and was able to right itself and fly into the ditch. I hadn't seen that happen since I was a teenager, when we used to find an adult to buy us a twelve-pack and we'd park along the highway to watch those chicken trucks fly by, our boredom at such a fever pitch we lived for those moments a chicken would escape, taking bets on which hawk would win the battle for dinner (macabre, I know, but such is the life of country kids used to animal deaths). And yet we could never shake our feelings of discontent, of being stuck somewhere we feared we'd never be able to leave.

An Essay

MYNA CHANG

"Blackberry Nights," began with an image of my grandmother, Belle. Every year, she spent an entire day pruning and shaping her rose bushes. The aggressive thorns gouged her paper-thin skin, leaving a tapestry of heavy scabs she called "the red death." I was repulsed by this physical evidence of her sacrifice to those plants. But I also loved the flowers—if the wind was fair, we would have a week of brilliant color and intoxicating fragrance. In the desiccated Oklahoma landscape, her garden seemed otherworldly. This memory put me in mind of the more profound burdens grandmothers and mothers and daughters are expected to endure for their families. I struggled to piece these images into a coherent story until I happened upon an article about the enchanting names of the full moons. This hint of moon magic gave me an abstract path into the story and a specu-lative mindset for building the atmosphere. One of my bad writing habits is to focus on language at the expense of clarity; knowing this, my next step was to excise and sharpen. I considered whether phrases such as "the fruit of my marrow" would deepen the story or instead muddy the arc. I cut a lot from my overwritten early drafts. Perhaps this is similar to the way my grandmother trimmed her unruly garden.

A random occurrence also helped me refine my first draft of "Hometown Johnnies." I wanted to capture the commoditization of impoverished boys and young men in the rural areas of the U.S. Dangerous jobs on oil rigs or grain elevators were the only choice for many; some, like the boy who would one day become my stepfather, were pressed into military service in lieu of finishing high school. The story idea crystallized during a Keanu Reeves movie marathon. I noted that many male movie characters are named John and they often seem interchangeable—that's when I realized the young man in my story couldn't be a singular character. He had to stand in for all the boys in my hometown, lacking the agency to inhabit a first-person point of view in his own story, his life unfolding in the view of the collective "we." A question from a critique partner led to the final step in editing: changing the title to the plural, "Johnnies."

Why I Write Short

SUZANNE HICKS

Would it surprise you to know that I do most of my writing on my cellphone? Good thing I write short! I didn't always use my phone as my primary writing tool, but among the many things that multiple sclerosis has affected is my dexterity. Using the dictation feature on my phone and typing with my thumbs has become my preferred way to get the words down. But I don't write short because it's easier on my hands; that's just how it worked out for me. It's what I've been writing even before I knew it had a name.

What I love most about writing short are the possibilities. Brevity isn't so much a constraint but an opportunity to get creative and try something different. It allows a writer to play with form in truly unique ways. Write the story backwards, turn it into an instructional guide, meld two narratives into one.

"What You Keep" and "Reservoir" share some commonalities. Both are driven by form. Both began in workshops, which can be a great place to pull out the ideas. Finally, both of these pieces have themes that are common in my writing: memory and place.

"What You Keep" was built around memory, specifically the main character's memories of special moments they shared with their grandmother. It serves as a meditation on how important these types of memories are to us. I chose to use the breathless paragraph format for this piece, which was new to me at the time. It felt like the right form for the story because it draws you into the main character's grief without pause. It allows for each moment to be stitched into a single thought.

"Reservoir" was inspired by place, specifically Las Vegas, Nevada, where I live. Again, form drove this piece as I started putting together these headlines of unlikely events happening in town. I wanted to tell a story about community, one that made the reader shift away from what typically comes to mind when thinking of Las Vegas. I tried to lean into the weird a bit, too, which was fun.

Some writers embrace both long and short forms. Some write prose and poetry. I venture between fiction and creative nonfiction, but it's always short. I'm a flash writer, and the micro is my sweet spot.

Best Microfiction thanks the journals where these pieces appeared in 2023.

All material used by permission.

"A Bird Has Grown Inside My Throat" by Mileva Anastasiadou and "Kin" by Mikki Aronoff from *Atlas and Alice*.

"1987" by Carolyn R. Russell from *Blink-Ink*.

"Blackberry Nights" by Myna Chang and "The Punch" by Tiffany Hsieh from *Cease, Cows*.

"Lace in Your Hands" by Lydia Gwyn and "Past Jack Koo's shop" by Frankie McMillan from *Centaur*.

"When He Heard about the Y2K Bug" by Addison Zeller from *The Cincinnati Review*.

"Mother Tongue" by Kik Lodge and "In Leaping" by Mandira Pattnaik from *The Citron Review*.

"Sacrament" by Melissa Llanes Brownlee and "Sibling Parenting" by Shih-Li Kow from *CRAFT*.

"Past Imperfect" by Louella Lester from *Cult. Magazine*.

"Lesson One: Simona" by Kati Bumbera , "Its Meanness to the World" by Jon Doughboy, "Reservoir" by Suzanne Hicks, and "When the Cowbirds Come to

Carry Your Sister Away" by Audra Kerr Brown from *The Disappointed Housewife.*

"Parallel" by Kelli Short Borges from *The Dribble Drabble Review.*

"We walked out of the forest" by Francine Witte from *The Ekphrastic Review.*

"Contortionists" by Keith J. Powell from *Emerge Literary Journal.*

"Our Mothers" by L Mari Harris from *Exposition Review.*

"Culloden" by Dawn Miller from *Fictive Dream.*

"Giant Silk Moth" by Angeline Schellenberg from *50-Word Stories.*

"Banana" by Laila Amado, "Dog People" by Abbie Barker, and "The Wives of Husbands in Space" by Aaron Sandberg from *Flash Frog.*

"The morendo" by Yedidyah Herrero and "A tiny, tiny bit of beauty" by Laila Miller from *Flash Frontier: An Adventure in Short Fiction.*

"Spinning" by Jude Higgins and "The No Longer Girls" by Jen Wyrauch Edson from *FlashFlood.*

"At A Roadside Attraction On The Brink Of Divorce" by Eric Scot Tryon from *The Forge Literary Magazine.*

"Hometown Johnnies" by Myna Chang from *Fractured Lit.*

"Father" by Alexandra Fössinger from *Full House Literary.*

"Make Me Yours" by Christine H. Chen and "Tangerine" by Allison Field Bell from *Ghost Parachute.*

"Not the End of the World" by Nan Wigington from *NUNUM*.

"October Again" by Beth Sherman and "Flemish Tavern" by Phillip Sterling from *100 Word Story*.

"Beautification" by Ken Poyner and "Proof" by Ken Poyner from *Open: Journal of Arts & Letters*.

"9/11 in Owensboro, Kentucky" by Thomas O'Connell from *Paragraph Planet*.

"Something Inside Us Rises Up" by L Mari Harris, "The Angel Gabriel Says It's Not a Booty Call If He Doesn't Have Genitals," by Frances Klein, and "Last Seen" by Eric Scot Tryon from *Peatsmoke Journal*.

"Danger Proximal" by Brett Biebel, "Maxillectomy" by Christine H. Chen, and "Flotsam" by Rebecca Turkewitz from *Pithead Chapel*.

"Method for a Sunday Roast" by Sian Meades-Williams from *The Prose Poem*.

"After Steady Work Dries Up, the Aging B-Movie Queen Reconsiders Fright Night" by Alyson Mosquera Dutemple from *Salamander*.

"Coyotes, Pelicans, & Prisoners" by Guy Biederman from *Six Sentences*.

"Stargazey Pie" by Rick White from *Splonk*.

"Lovesong for the 0% Finance King Size Mattress" by Jo Gatford from *Stanchion*.

"Chopsticks" by Jeff Friedman from *Switch*.

"Dead Girl Summer" by Saumya Sawant from *Tint Journal*.

"Snow, 1979" by Alan Beard and "Bones, Only Bones" by Frances Gapper from *trampset*.

"Pastels" by Nicole Brogdon and "One Fell Off" by Keith Hood from *Vestal Review*.

"Exorcism" by Sara Henry Paolozzi and "Pancakes" by Kristin Tenor from *Wigleaf*.

"Genie" by Kip Knott from *Wrong Turn Lit*.

"Mulberries" by Jon Doughboy, "Hive" by Kelli Short Borges, and "There is No Gold Here" by Elena Zhang from *Your Impossible Voice*.

112 Harvard Ave #65
Claremont, CA 91711 USA

pelekinesis@gmail.com
www.pelekinesis.com

Pelekinesis titles are available through Ingram,
Gardners, directly from the publisher's website,
and at your favorite local bookstore.

www.ingramcontent.com/pod-product-compliance
Lightning Source LLC
Chambersburg PA
CBHW031955010726
47493CB00007B/2207